The Battle of Otter Tail County

THE BATTLE

OF

OTTER TAIL COUNTY

JACK LAMBERT

NORTH STAR PRESS OF ST. CLOUD, INC.

St. Cloud, Minnesota

To my beloved Dolly,
partner for 55 years in all things
and still the wind in my sails.

ISBN: 0-87839-367-6
ISBN-13: 978-0-87839-367-1

First Edition, September 1, 2010

Printed in the United States of America

Published by
North Star Press of St. Cloud, Inc.
P.O. Box 451
St. Cloud, Minnesota 56302

www.northstarpress.com

TEN MILE LAKE

ONE

THE DOORFRAME OF THE OLD house near St. Paul's Swede Hollow shattered as four hooded young toughs burst in about midnight. The gang members intercepted Rolf Holt as he limped from his bed. He was immediately floored by the stroke of an aluminum bat alongside his right knee. The four hovered over him while they all shouted, "Money! Give us the money, man!"

"Does this look like a bank?" Holt was down but unbowed.

The gang leader kicked him in the ribs and shouted, "We know you got money, old man. We seen you walking to Payne Avenue all the time." Rolf worked in an auto garage on Payne, shopped the street for his meager needs and occasionally visited the American Legion club, sufficient evidence of assumed wealth to their terminal stupidity.

"Here's his wallet," another punk said triumphantly, handing it to the leader.

"Shit! There's only fifteen dollars here. No credit cards." An angry kick struck the downed man.

"He must have money hidden somewhere. Tear the fucking place apart." They went about their work enthusiastically, overturning the mattress, pulling out and dumping drawers. One ran up to the second floor and another checked the basement. While the fruitless search was maturing into wanton vandalism, the leader dropped his bat and pulled a snub nose

1

revolver from his pocket. Pointing it at the old man he demanded to know where he kept his hoard.

His face screwed up in pain, Rolf forced out, "Rolf Holt, Staff Sergeant, Serial Number 36233264."

"What's that mean? You old bastard!" Another kick. The old man crouched in a corner. He wanted to stand but his right knee telegraphed that it might not be wise. Still he divulged nothing, remaining silent and defiant.

"Man, you gonna die if you don't talk." The leader brandished the revolver a few inches from his face as the others rampaged noisily through the house.

Rolf just shook his head and forced a grin, meeting the masked man eye to eye. "The German Army couldn't kill me, and I doubt that you have the balls. Hell, I've killed better men than you." A pistol whipping followed, as the leader worked himself into a frenzy. Still the old man failed to be cowed but rather displayed a sneering disrespect.

Finally the accomplices rallied to say that they could find nothing of value but a couple of old shotguns in the basement. Otherwise there was no salable loot among the Spartan furnishings or the sort of goods suitable for fencing to a pawnshop: no jewelry, no electronic gear, and no coin or stamp collections.

The leader was trying to summon his resolve to kill the unarmed old man when they heard the sirens. There was a St. Paul police precinct station just a few blocks away. A neighbor, hearing the racket, had called 911. The courage of the mob began to evaporate, some already gravitating toward the back door. The pistolero hesitated, angry but slightly mesmerized by the old man's unblinking courage, then he too ran.

The first squad of officers launched a futile pursuit, but darkness easily swallowed the hoodlums. The second pair attended the victim before an ambulance took the protesting elder to Regions General Hospital. He had taken a beating but the wounds were largely superficial.

The police offered to have Ramsey County Community Services assist him with the cleanup of his home, but Rolf declined all help except the temporary boarding of his smashed back door. He got his Colt .45 caliber automatic pistol down from a shelf in the bedroom closet, where it had luckily gone undetected, and put it on the small nightstand by his bed, not intending to be surprised a second time. While he was still cleaning and repairing the house, I called him. Rolf and I, Mike Odell, had been friends for a very long time.

JUST A FEW DAYS LATER THE TWO ELDERS watched a twilight display of unparalleled beauty from Mike's Minnesota lake cabin. The rays of the setting July sun, probing through ribbons of stratocumulus clouds, like God's air-brush, progressively painted soft pastels of yellow-gold to red, lavender, and finally deep purple that spawned the night. The panorama was reflected in duplicate on the nearly still waters of South Ten Mile Lake. Only a northbound squadron of geese and a pair of trolling fishermen intruded on the sublime scene so common to the Minnesota lake country.

"Welcome to Geezerville," I said. "This is one of my primary recreational activities."

Rolf said nothing, and I refrained from intruding on his thoughts—a guy thing—didn't spoil it with talk. However, it was his first day here, and I couldn't help but ponder his state of mind. He held a beer in his left hand and a cigar in his right and gazed seemingly transfixed toward the west, like it was a movie screen, and he might miss the climax. They couldn't view sunsets like this from the closely packed houses of the smoggy inner city. And while it was standard fare for me, the quiet beauty and serenity were remarkable for him. No shouting, no screeching tires, no boom boxes.

I had moved Rolf just that day from the St. Paul home he had occupied for nearly three-fourths of a century, to my cabin on Ten Mile Lake near Fergus Falls, Minnesota. He had come reluctantly, but had finally been obliged to accept that his old home in St. Paul was a well of loneliness and isolation in what had become a foreign land.

Despite the break-in and mugging Rolf had suffered at the hands of gang punks, he had planned to tough it out in the old family house. One of my periodic phone calls to my friend of more than sixty years had started his move to the lake. The tone of voice—the pain and despair—was something I had never heard from this tough Norwegian. He had weathered World War II and life's catalogue of domestic and personal failures without seeming to be defeated. Grumpy but never defeated.

Rolf was one of that legion of citizen soldiers who did his duty, faced death, then faded, unsung, into the obscurity of post war life with its montage of modest successes and mulitple defeats. He had survived combat in Europe but had been a victim of Murphy's Law in later life. Murphy had declared that what could go wrong would go wrong. And there were many who considered Murphy a raging optimist.

I had visited the Holt home near Swede Hollow on St. Paul's east side many times. Though modest, it had been a nice two-story house in a neat, blue-collar neighborhood. But in the mid-1990s things had changed. Many houses were badly maintained, front porches sagged with junk, and most yards were untended. Gang symbols and graffiti dominated the alleyways. The once proud neighborhood now had an air of desperate shabbiness. Fifty years ago this community had provided solid workers for the railroads, 3M, Whirlpool, and the Hamm Brewery. Most of those businesses had consolidated, relocated or vanished, and the good-paying jobs went with them. Five decades later the stable old guard had largely passed on, their grown children had moved away, and a seedier element had seeped into the neighborhood.

Rolf's wife, Ella, had beaten the corporate exodus by several decades. She'd abandoned him and returned to Georgia with their infant son in 1949, berating him for his reluctance to change his occupation or location. He had been a millwright with top hourly wages, and that was the sort of work he wanted to do, what he was good at. And he had an ill, aging mother to care for. Apart from that responsibility, this son of the Great Depression could not understand taking a chance and changing his line of work or his steady job at a machine shop. Stability was what he already had, something considered sacred by his Norwegian parents, whose families had been immigrants. You didn't chuck stability for an uncertain future in a strange place. Besides he had taken his military training in Georgia and disliked the area just as much as Ella had come to hate Minnesota. So when she said she was going back to Georgia with the baby for a visit, Rolf paid her way, hoping that she would return but fearing that she might not.

He had written to Ella and sent her money as he dealt with his job and bed-ridden mother, whom he buried five years later. The following years slipped by as he doggedly marched to his gritty jobs. The machine shop closed in the sixties, but he was able to sign on as a maintenance man with a conveyor-manufacturing firm. But that company merged and the plant closed in the seventies. Still he clung to his little single-family home, working at nearby garages and small engine repair shops. He wasn't particularly happy at the old house, but it was paid for, it seemed to suit him, and there was the gnawing concern that this place might be the only possible link to his missing son. If he left, that connection was broken. Besides, he could live there on his modest income. All that seemed sufficient reason to resist change until the night that gang shattered his solitude. They'd seen him hobbling along Payne Avenue. His right knee was failing and made him look feebler than he was.

So when they broke into the house through the back door they had not expected the old codger to do anything but cower in a corner. Rolf had tried to go for his pistol but was jumped before he could get it into play.

MY ROUTINE CALL TO HIM WAS JUST three days after he had been patched up at the hospital. "Ahc," he muttered in his gravely voice, "I've been through worse. I would've defended myself if that damn right knee of mine hadn't buckled before I could get to my pistol." Rolf had seen combat in Europe in World War II and would have been a fierce opponent if his .45 had been unlimbered in time.

I drove to St. Paul immediately and told my friend that he should put this part of his life behind him and come to live with me at my lake place. He had visited me at Ten Mile Lake once when it was still a summer cabin, and enjoyed it, but, like me, he had become mired in the familiarity of his own tiny sphere. His range of activity had been further restricted when he sold his car, providing an excuse for not going much beyond the old neighborhood. The decision to go pedestrian had been eco-nomic and coincided with the loss of his modest health insur-ance. Part-time work at an auto repair shop was just three blocks away. No need of a car or the obligatory liability insurance.

I was shocked at Rolf's appearance. We usually stood eye to eye, but he seemed to have sagged down and to starboard, like an old boat left too long in the water. His bruised face had been repaired in the emergency room but the scars were fresh, stitches showing, and caused me to wince. He read my reaction and was humiliated at being found in such a condition.

"Ahc, what would I do up there?" he protested.

"Fish, hunt, chop wood, shoot the bull, wallow in tranquility. What do you do here?" I responded. He pondered in silence and a quizzical, introspective look brushed across his face. He maintained his small house, watched the Twins and Vikings on an ancient, rabbit-eared TV set (too old and heavy for even the thieves), ate badly, and shopped and worked along Payne Avenue, content with a peripheral role in life.

"Not very damn much," was his response. But the idea of moving seemed to overwhelm him. I explained that we could find someone to dispose of his furnishings at an estate sale and put the house in the hands of a real estate agent. He could walk away. They would mail him the proceeds.

"What the hell is keeping you here?" I asked.

Rolf Holt was not the kind of person to give up easily. He clung to the house and its memories, mostly bad and mostly fading. "For a long time, I kept thinking Ella and my son might come back, but I know that's a pipe dream. Arnie, Arnold was my little boy's name, after my father. (He forgot that I had been the infant's godfather.) How would they find me if I moved? I wouldn't much care to see her, but my son . . ." He shook his head as if pondering the dilemma of a small child standing on the doorstep seeking his long-lost father.

"He's a grown man now, making his way in the world," I stated the obvious. Something he already knew.

After two days of anguish for Rolf and arrangements for the house, we began to assemble bags of his clothing including a faded old Army duffel bag that still bore his stenciled name. There was also a pitiful collection of memorabilia in a cardboard box: A photo of his deceased parents, a candid shot of him in uniform, another of Ella holding an infant, his Colt .45 and some papers. A toolbox, and a rarely used fishing tackle box, rounded out his pile of personal "stuff."

He never looked back at his house, but as I aimed my Ford pickup toward Fergus Falls, Rolf proclaimed, "But I won't be a burden on anyone. Not even my best friend," a thought he had obviously been nurturing. It was rendered like a final warning.

"When you get to be a burden, I'll use that .45 on you." The slightest suggestion of a smile peeked out amidst his bruises.

Indeed the old Army issue Colt would play a role in our future that I could never have foreseen.

TWO

ROLF AND I WERE NOT EXACTLY matched bookends—he a blond, blue-eyed, chiseled-featured descendant of Vikings, resembling an old Clint Eastwood, and me a dark haired, brown-eyed, rumpled-faced son of Irish stock. "Irish as Patty's Pig" my mother used to say. Our grandparents had all been immigrants. But our life experiences had some remarkable similarities as we grew up around St. Paul's east side. Both of our fathers worked for the railroads. My family attended Trinity Catholic Church and the Holts went to St. John's Lutheran just two blocks away.

We first met at Johnson High School and had chummed around since we were fifteen. I had been a mediocre left fielder and a poor hitter. Rolf was a fine athlete who had played end on the varsity football team and had run the dashes and hurdles on the track team. Right after graduation in 1943, we had joined the Army together. Couldn't wait to get into the fight, exuberant in our youthful stupidity. On enlistment at Fort Snelling, an aged officer had assured us that we could stay together. Almost immediately orders sent me to an air base in Texas and Rolf to an infantry-training center in Georgia. He went to Europe seeing several months of bitter ground combat, while I became a tail gunner on a B-24 bound for the Pacific. Rolf had mechanical skills and ended up digging foxholes. I didn't have a shot glass full of mechanical aptitude and was assigned technical training on armaments and a job surrounded by paraphernalia. Such were the ways of the United States military with its wealth of manpower that made it disdainful of individual talent.

Courtesy of Uncle Sugar, I became one of those cocky, tanned young gods seen in era photos with the wave of hair peeking out from under a variety of saucy military headgear, standing next to a great silver war bird.

Both of us survived the war, though Rolf's service was tough and mine was a relative lark, and returned to St. Paul in 1946. Rolf had been missing in action for a short time and the telegram notifying his parents had precipitated his father's heart attack. Rolf survived but his father died before the son's return from the war.

Back home we renewed our friendship and concentrated on further education, courtesy of the G.I. bill, and cared for our aging parents. Rolf went to vocational school. I went to the University of Minnesota. The big difference in our lives at this juncture was that Rolf had brought home a southern war bride, a pregnant one at that. She delivered in due course, and I was one of the godparents at the christening for little Arnie along with Rolf's Aunt Hattie who hailed from North Dakota.

From our first acquaintance, Ella seemed aloof. For Rolf's sake I tried to be pleasant. I was his friend, not a rival. She had a disapproving sort of sneer on her face for me, maybe for everyone, which spoiled her otherwise good looks. She was one of those domineering souls unable to accommodate others. In fairly short order, she voiced her unhappiness with her living conditions, the town, the climate, and the tendency of Rolf and me to quaff a few at a local pub. A staunch Baptist, despite the hard drinking of her father, or perhaps because of it, Ella was aghast at the thought of our imbibing. When I dropped by to suggest that Rolf and I might go down to the Legion Club and "tip a few," she challenged, "Might you be considering alcoholic beverages?" She rolled out the word "alcoholic" like it was number one on God's "thou-shalt-not" list and accompanied the inquisition with dramatic eye bugging.

My response, "That's exactly what I had in mind," did nothing to elevate my status with her and managed to make Rolf's life a little tougher.

"Why don't you just say we're going to a meeting at the Legion or out for an ice cream cone?" he later admonished.

Frankly, I wondered how Rolf had gotten cozy enough with the ornery Ella to manage any romance. But then, youthful passion and logic were never synonymous. He had not dated in high school, was pretty shy around girls. He was good-looking and must have been fatally attractive in his uniform. And she may have seen him as an avenue of escape from her own roots.

"Those people of Ella's went to church all day Sunday," he had once told me. "And in between Sundays her mother was constantly yammering about sin. She never gave her mouth a rest. That old pickelpuss could talk the bark off a tree.

"The only sinning I saw thereabouts was by Ella's Pa and her uncle. They drank moonshine in the barn and talked about harassing Negroes and avoiding work. Both were in the Klan. The uncle said he was an Infernal Lizard, or some such. Wanted me to join, said I was Aryan stock. Neither of them ever fought a war, but they were hell on wheels when it came to blacks. Hell, blacks bled just like the rest of us in Europe. I hated it down there, couldn't wait to leave. Those people argued, didn't get along with each other, much less outsiders. Ella seemed anxious to leave too. I encouraged her. Be better away from those battling rednecks."

"No loyalty," he later said when referring to his wife's departure. Loyalty was a recurring theme with Rolf, at the core of his own personal philosophy, although he wasn't one to hold forth on such matters. It meant perseverance in the face of adversity, clinging to principles, doing the right thing and going down with the ship if it came to that. Rolf was that rare type who never spared himself, never chose the easy road, only the honorable way, which is often the hard path.

MY OWN ATTEMPT AT MARRIAGE had been a similar train wreck. I held off until I had managed to graduate with an education major and a history minor. During my first year of teaching, I had married Karen. Wedded bliss was short, less than three years.

Karen, a blonde, blue-eyed Venus with a vibrant personality, lit up a gathering where women gave her that critical "dumb bimbo" look and men tried not to let their wives see them stare.

However, great looks and charm masked a relentless ambition attached to a viper-like tongue. All of which she kept pretty well camouflaged during our courtship. She was certain in her convictions and incapable of keeping them to herself. Discussion quickly became argument, and careless insults that could not be recalled were frequent.

Karen had a secretarial job at 3M and immediately began campaigning for me to abandon teaching for business. She wanted to move up in the world and mapped ways in which we might both climb the social ladder. I was also nagged to get my masters (something I did in my own time), apply for a position at 3M, try for the state legislature. Her lash was applied consistently. And she was forever arranging weekend social dos when I wanted to fish, hunt, or just relax. Karen not only refused to bait a hook she wouldn't get near a lake. Incompatible was our middle name.

She kept throwing the ambition challenge in my face. I thought surviving the war, putting myself through college, and helping my aging parents was as much as I could say grace over for the time being. And I felt that in time I could change Karen. You come to believe—you kid yourself—that you can remold the mindset of others.

She morphed into an ice queen, rationing her sexual goodies as an inducement for me to follow her master plan. It reminded me of how Father Moore had withheld gym privileges at Trinity School to punish all of us for the alleged sins of a few or to insure our future good behavior. And, believe me, there was a lot of guilt among fourteen-year-old boys, though little sinning. Inevitably Karen and I divorced, and my ears got a rest from the din of criticism. She went off to bag some unsuspecting businessman.

My Gaelic charm led me to dates, but the Karen experience left me jaundiced regarding marriage. So I dodged commitment to anyone but myself until I was too old to be eligible, too old to be wanted and too old to care.

Like Rolf, I had ill parents to care for and did my duty to them until they had passed on by the mid-1960s, then I moved into an apartment and eventually got my masters degree.

Throughout this time, Rolf stuck with the old Holt house on the East Side. He never made money to salt away, but paid the mortgage, and just kept plugging along, reluctant to take a chance. While Rolf concentrated on his occupation as a mechanic, I busied myself with teaching history and social studies. However, we often met on weekends to down a few beers, and went on rare duck hunt and fishing expeditions, spending the day together in a boat or a duck blind, enjoying each other's company, saying no more than a few words.

I was fairly gabby, an Irish trait, but Rolf was your basic detached, stoic Norwegian. He was a deep thinker, and when he spoke it was with sparse, well-chosen words.

Some of our Johnson High classmates had become men of prominence—judges, captains of industry. But our post World War II lives had been strikingly unremarkable. We just bumbled along taking the path of least resistance. Suddenly, or so it seemed, all our crossroads of opportunity were in the rear-view mirror. We were a couple of old duffers, reflecting on our catalog of mistakes, paths not taken.

"She wasn't loyal," said Rolf, "leaving and taking my son. I sent money for him and tried to stay in touch, but after a couple of years lost contact. My checks were coming back with a funny endorsement, and then after a time I couldn't reach her by phone. Phone disconnected, letters returned by the post office. I reached her uncle once, and he said he didn't know where she was, wasn't her keeper. But then I should have done something. I don't know what exactly, but I wasn't loyal to my son."

He said all this looking out over the windshield at I-94, as we unreeled his connections to St. Paul.

Words failed me for a change. I struggled to say something adequate that didn't look like criticim for difficult decisions of fifty years ago. God knows Ella was a disagreeable bitch. And it sounded as if she had taken advantage of his good nature by accepting money with no intention of returning. So I just kept quiet out of respect for his deep feelings. Rolf was not in need of talk. He was just voicing his ruminations.

As we continued toward Fergus Falls, Rolf was silent for a long time, cogitating. He had been mired in the familiarity of his own cocoon for too long, unhappy, but reluctant to break out. Finally he asked me about my neighbors.

"Minnesota nice is trite. They're solid, reserved, salt-of-the-earth folks. We don't have any full-time neighbors who live real close by. Not like in the city. A good many of the places are just summer homes." That might have been more than he wanted to know, but I wanted him to feel at ease.

"Any crime up there, " Rolf asked some time later.

"An occasional winter break-in at a closed cabin, a few scalawags, but nothing serious."

Another half hour passed. "I didn't like the way the people on my street were acting. They talked loud, played those car stereos so loud I could hear them in my house with the windows closed and the TV on. All going to be deaf as stumps by the time they're thirty. And it isn't even music, just a bunch of racket."

"Well I've got a stereo and tapes at the cabin," I responded, "but all you'll hear is good old jazz and swing, by those great folks we grew up with—Benny Goodman, the Dorseys, Glenn Miller. You know."

"All dead," Rolf accurately noted.

"So are we, almost. But the lyrics are great, and you can understand the words."

"Just a repetitive racket," Rolf said, by a roundabout way of agreeing, "that's what the music is now. That rap crap is even worse. On TV those rappers are dressed like they just fell off the back of the turnip wagon and jump around like they have squirrels in their shorts." I took that as confirmation that my taste in music would not clash with his.

Changing the subject I asked, "What sort of people were these gang members?

"Hooded," was his curt reply.

"But could you determine their race? White, Asian, Blacks, Latinos?"

"Spics I think. Damn sombitches."

Rolf was never a jolly type, but the years of loneliness capped by the mugging had left him bitter and negative. I had my work cut out for me.

THREE

IN THE LATE 1980S, AFTER HAVING hunted and fished in West Central Minnesota for many years, I had indulged myself, buying a small summer cabin off Interstate 94 on Ten Mile Lake in Otter Tail County. Dalton was a close-by crossroads village, but Fergus Falls (just Fergus to the natives) was the county seat, a town some fifteen minutes away. The pretty little community of 12,000 was named after James Fergus, a descendent of Scottish royalty and a prairie entrepreneur from Little Falls, Minnesota. In 1856 he risked his capital, but not his scalp, to finance trapper-adventurer, Joe Whitford. A man of bold vision but limited instincts, Joe contemplated economic development in the wilds of Western Minnesota despite the prior claims of the Native American population. He was a visionary, born several decades too soon. The only attraction in this forsaken wilderness was a falls on the Otter Tail River. It held the potential for waterpower, necessary to operate a sawmill and gristmill, essential to a pioneer settlement. Despite Whitford's subsequent death at the hands of Sioux Indians, Northern Europeans braved the new land. A dam, optimizing the natural waterpower, was built ten years later and the railroad followed in another ten. James Fergus never fell here, nor did he take up residence, no doubt sobered by Whitford's experience.

VISITING WEEKENDS AND SUMMERS, I began to make the modifications necessary for year-round living. I insulated and paneled adequately despite my propensity to measure once and cut twice. With no devotion toward my rented digs in the Cities, I had dreamed longingly of the lake cabin as my reward from a life of limited accomplishment.

My abdication after some forty years of teaching, although I had loved helping young people discover the past that would shape the future, was easier than I thought it would be. First of all, I had developed a longing for the lake country home.

Secondly, I had begun to weary of the kids' drift toward whininess and their lack of self-discipline. "It's not fair" and "It sucks" were a constant refrain by these alleged leaders of the future who had known neither war nor poverty. Despite my attempts to cram some history into them, most didn't know Pearl Harbor from Pearl Bailey. And for many students, my emphasis on the Constitution, the structural foundation of our well ordered society, was met with bored indifference.

Then, like the plague, there began the incessant staff and PTA meetings over non-education issues: diversity training, grading regardless of achievement, litigation concerns, and discipline issues, the litany that seemed to be dominating schooling.

Rather than going with the flow, I had reacted belligerently and had become unpopular among my fellow faculty members, most pointedly the English teachers, for my oft-expressed opinions about the inability of students to communicate. "*You know*," "*I mean*," and "*like*," repeated over and over, had become words that permeated their vocabulary and frustrated their writing ability.

"No, I don't *know*." I would taunt a student. "Use your brain and explain with suitable words. And do not say '*like*' again. The

War Between the States was not *like* a civil war, it *was* a civil war." A few kids worked to articulate. Many were just pasturing. For them I was just an aging impediment on their stroll toward mediocrity. I was too old to accommodate such linguistic fads and losing whatever tolerance I once possessed.

What also pushed me toward the door was the decline in student standards of conduct (permitted by a docile school administration). The inmates had begun taking over the asylum. From, a consistent, "Yes, Mr. Odell," things had regressed until a final, "Like, you know, fuck you man." This from an unclean bozo wearing the crotch of his pants between his knees and festooned with enough piercings that it seemed he might spring a leak all over his black costume.

Before a disciplinary hearing, I told the Goth wannabe that he sounded like an illiterate jackass. "A simple, fuck you," I said, would have been sufficient to express his point and more grammatical. The principal was not amused by either of us.

The final straw came during a faculty-administration conference about history curriculum. Some had deemed it time to modify history. People I had never heard of were present. One young lady was introduced as the District director of Ethnicity. No kidding. There was a lot of wishy-washy talk about how we presented World War II. Korea was unknown to most of these intellectuals, and they were all in the Jane Fonda camp as regards Vietnam. Few of them had ever served in the military. Truman's decision to drop the A-bombs on Japan surfaced in considering a Smithsonian display of the *Enola Gay*. Next year's senior class trip would be to D.C. I ventured the opinion that making the *Enola Gay* project about Japanese suffering was rank revisionism. Eyes rolled, and a young pasty-faced faculty member made the mistake of saying that I didn't have my facts straight on who did the real killing. I rose to the bait: "Hell, I was there, and you weren't born yet." The debate escalated when the twerp jumped up, stuck his finger in my face and dubbed me a warmonger. I offered to hit him so hard he'd smell bad for a week.

Most of my faculty contemporaries were already cashing their pension checks and the few that remained treated me like Typhoid Mary. There was no, "Goodbye Mister Chips." party.

So I took the plunge and signed my retirement papers, although advised that my early death would be beneficial to the plan because a substantial portion of teachers' future retirement was underfunded. One more "gotcha" from the establishment:

Retiring to the lake, with my dog Bo, rid me of all the aggravations of the educational system. I was also brain weary from my sense that the study of history, which I had revered, now seemed irrelevant. There had been two world wars to give order and a sense of brotherhood to humanity. I had participated in the last of them. And yet there was no peace despite the volume of rhetoric at the United Nations. Conflict abounded. Now the Muslim world was warring against Judeo-Christians, rekindling the animosities of many centuries earlier, babbling about jihad. They were still pissed about the crusades, and they'd won that war. Sore winners. The Arabs are as bad as the Irish. Despite all the lessons of history the world is still mired in religious/tribal warfare.

The whole business left me profoundly frustrated. I was tired-old: different than being tired and young from exercise, a job, the prom, sex.

Unlike the hermit on the mountain, I retreated from the world not to seek wisdom but into ignoble isolation. Writing an occasional history article for military journals and cussing the TV news filled the intellectual void. I exercised by working on the cabin, mowing the grass, chopping firewood, and horsing around with Bo. Hunting and fishing, in season, were my only scheduled activities. But mostly I just sat and gazed at the lake from my cabin or my boat, nestling further into my, "island-valley of Avilion." It had a certain serene sameness, yet the sky, the land, and lake was ever changing: like watching the symphony of flames in a fireplace. This place seemed to define me in my old age.

Although I was about to share the cabin with Rolf, I found that I was strangely apprehensive regarding his approval. After all, he had few options now that I had dragooned him into my world.

I was relieved when he first looked about the house and said, "Good workmanship." It was high praise from a craftsman. His only other visit had been five years ago before my improvements, when he still had a car. Others had referred to it as my fishing shack. Indeed the sole decorative furnishing was a large, limited-edition Peter Maas rendering of canvasback ducks settling into a spread of decoys. But Rolf's appraisal made the house seem less shacky. And the curtainless windows and spare nature of the decorations, as befits a bachelor's den, suited Rolf's Spartan sense of style.

My one-story lake home, raised a half level by a building block foundation, contained two small but ample bedrooms, bathroom, utility room, kitchen and a room that I grandly referred to as "the Great Room." The latter wasn't all that vast, but served as the combined foyer, kitchen, dining room, parlor, and general lollygagging-about-room. An L-shaped west-facing deck on the lake and south side also provided some additional living area in good weather. A boat dock, unattached garage, and a propane tank, the latter resembling a beached whale, completed the layout. I had about 100 feet of lakeshore with some nice cottonwoods on the lot corners.

The nearest neighboring structures on either side were ancient house trailers that hadn't seen the road in thirty years and rarely ever saw an occupant except for summer week-ends. A pair of old folks, who I believed were in ill health, owned the trailer to the north. I'd not seen them for over a year. A nice couple, professors at the University of Minnesota, owned the one to the south. Last year they told me that they would be gone on a sabbatical to the Holy Land. There were a few other permanent residents nearby, but none to intrude on my solitude. Two lots to the south was a first-class two-story house owned by my friends, retirees Paul and Ida Hansen.

People hereabouts, though friendly to a fault, practiced minding their own business. If you indicated a willingness to chat they were gregarious but not pushy. If there were any radical elements intent on imposing their extreme drivel, I had yet to encounter them. They were all down in the cities I guessed.

The day after Rolf arrived I took him for breakfast at the Dalton Cafe, a tiny place where strangers stood out like buffalo but were warmly greeted. I was acquainted with one or two customers and the owner-waitress who must have wondered about my battered companion but resisted asking if he had fallen off a bar stool. We ate a thrashing crew's breakfast because I had cautioned Rolf that pouring it out of a box or a bottle was my normal routine.

Actually, we were en route to the Fergus hospital for a little follow-up repair on Rolf's face. The bruises were getting better and the swelling was receding, but the legacy of the pistol whipping was a half dozen stitches on his skull and four more on his left cheekbone, and they gave signs of needing to be removed. The ER at Fergus was expert at fishhook removal so stitches were a snap. His Medicare paid for some of the service and I attempted to quietly cover the rest. However, Rolf caught me in the act and started to raise a ruckus.

"Ahc, I told you I didn't want to be a problem. I won't have it, Mike." But he didn't have the extra eighty dollars in cash that was on the hospital bill.

"Well they won't put the stitches back," I said, "so let me handle it. Next time I'll take out the stitches with my Rapala gutting knife."

My attempt at humor didn't take. "Tell me what it is and I'll pay you back." A proud, independent man this Rolf Holt.

Before we left the ER I had urged Rolf to get an X-ray of his right knee that he had been favoring. "Ahc, that isn't anything. I had it before that scuffle. It's just a bit of arthritis." The way he pronounced it was two words, like a person's name: "Arthur Ritis."

"Well, if it gets any worse, you should have it looked at. You got a hitch in your git-along."

"Ahc. Nothing."

Lacking supplemental insurance I knew that he would resist medical care like a tiger.

The trip into Fergus Falls provided an opportunity for him to see the town, and a prosperous farming community it was. "No crime hereabouts," Rolf declared after a brief tour that showed a neat and seemingly orderly community.

We got a fishing pole for him at the new Walmart, which had triggered the process of boutiquing Main Street, bought some food, and headed back to the lake for some promised angling.

I exited I-94 at Minnesota 59 and turned south through gently rolling farmland that was lush with corn, wheat, and soybeans. At County 35 we turned east to intercept Ten Mile Lake. Soon after the turn, Rolf declared, "My people were here."

"What?"

"There's a sign we just passed says, 'Viking Trail.'"

I had never noticed it. "What were the Vikings doing here?"

"Passing through," Rolf declared without hesitation.

Was he pulling my leg?

"Don't you know about the rune stone they found around here?"

"Oh, that," I said with more than a little skepticism in my tone.

"Well," Rolf bored ahead without a hint of humor, "everyone knows they came here long before Columbus."

"Not much question that they came to North America first" (after pillaging Ireland I thought), "but I doubt they made it this far."

"The rune stone says they were here," he persisted.

Reluctant to pick a fight on this issue or any other, I changed the subject, pointing out the lake view. We had just reached a high vista at the northwest corner of Ten Mile Lake. The homes on the west side spread down a road to our right. Morningside Drive it was called. (My road on the east shore should have been named Eveningside Drive but for reasons beyond me was dubbed Bankers Drive.) The view of the South Lake was quite beautiful as we descended to where the road passed between the lakes at the Ten Mile Lake Resort.

The closer we got to the cabin Rolf noticed that I was waving back at others we passed on the road. "Who are all those folks?" he asked.

"Oh, I don't know them all. But people up here do that. They're just being neighborly."

South Ten Mile was a substantial body of water, about a mile across and over a mile long. At the south end it narrowed into a bay of reeds ending at a small dam that held the lake at a respectable level in periods of drought. The best walleye fishing was at the mouth of the bay, short of the reed bank, not far from my east shore cabin.

Rolf lumbered into my fourteen-foot boat with some grunts but looked happy to be on the water in pursuit of the wily pike. Fishing is a sublime enterprise that requires some limited concentration and promises cheap thrills. That tug you feel in your fingertips could be a lunker or just a weed, but the anticipation is delicious, a fine way to forget the troubles of the world or your own personal demons. But Rolf couldn't quite shake his.

After baiting our hooks with fat minnows, we trolled the south end of Ten Mile Lake. Absent any prompt Rolf announced, "They ought to give those sombitches fire arms training." We had all come home from the service cursing like stable sergeants, but Rolf had never been a cusser. Sombitch was, I believe, the harshest curse I ever heard from him.

He was ruminating again, but I was too nonplused to focus on the subject for a second, and he went on as if in answer to the question I hadn't asked. "Mike, they don't know how to hold a gun or aim it. They do what's called "drive-by" shootings and usually just hit bystanders or knock holes in pizza parlors. If they were trained, they might do a better job of killing each other."

"Cleaning up the gene pool?" I suggested. He gave a satisfied nod toward my end of the boat.

Perhaps it was too warm and the fish were cooling at the bottom, since we got no action. Still I found it restful to contemplate the lines trailing in the water astern of the boat and imagine the walleye pike that was scrutinizing our bait. However, Rolf's mind was still back at the house in St. Paul reliving the break-in and beating. For a guy who rarely got up a first wind, Rolf was cranking up a second.

"All those wingnuts want is money for drugs. And all I had in my wallet was about fifteen dollars. So they took my Browning pump and an old shot gun that had been my dad's."

His face turned from bitter to a sly grin as he went on. "Dad's was a double barrel, one of those old Damascus spun-steel jobs. An antique. You can't fire modern loads in them or they'll come unraveled. I told the cops to watch for some jack-ass who showed up at the emergency room with his nose spread back to his ears. It would be the punk who took that old 12-gauge."

Suddenly I got a strike, and Rolf quickly reeled in to keep the hooked fish from tangling our lines. As I worked the catch alongside the boat, Rolf took charge of the landing net. It was a nice walleye, and I was a bit too anxious. Just as we thought the fish was played out, it spotted that landing net dipping into the water, jumped once then dove under the boat quickly, snapping the line on my trolling motor.

"Aw, shit!" I yelled loud enough for the entire lake to hear.

But the adventure invigorated Rolf, who let out the first laugh I had heard from him in some time. "Nice going, Mike. What a great fish. We'll get him next time."

As I began to re-rig my line, my disappointment was tempered by Rolf's pleasure. "How long has it been since you fished?" I asked.

He had to think for a minute as he cast his line back in the lake. "It may have been up here four or five years ago."

As it often does, the commotion with that lunker and the noise of our voices carrying over the water caused other boats to edge our way in subtle fashion. Close neighbors and good friends, Paul and Ida Hansen, came within hailing distance. They had seen our action and witnessed our failure. "Don't worry, I'll get him for you," Paul shouted as they trolled past. Their black Labrador, Tina, stood at the prow, as if navigating, tongue out, tail going furiously.

"Who's your friend?" asked Ida, a beautiful grandmother.

"I brought my grandfather to the lake," I said, and everyone chuckled, as we were all of an age. Rolf enjoyed it the most and laughed hard enough that he was obliged to wipe a tear from his eye. The thought of my old high school chum being my grandfather tickled the hell out of me too. For some time we shared silent nodding grins. It was a moment that could be spoiled by talk.

Back to the job of steering the boat and watching our trailing lines, I realized that I was relishing Rolf's companionship more than I had anticipated. I also felt a bit noble about rescuing him from the evils that had invaded the old neighborhood. I fancied that we could now live out our lives in obscure tranquility in this bit of paradise. But there was no evading fate. We remained in its crosshairs.

FOUR

I CONTINUED MY CHORES ABOUT the cabin, and Rolf just sort of merged into the drill routine. While I mowed the grass of three yards to a gnat's eyebrow, denying habitat to mosquitoes. Rolf puttered about the garage or stocked firewood. Common features of every lakeshore lot are close-cropped grass and a giant high-rise birdhouse for purple martins. Both helped to control the state bird, the mosquito. Since the occupants of the adjoining properties were never there I mowed their places in my unremitting war against the pest.

When I got off the John Deere riding mower, Rolf fell on it for maintenance and repairs that I had neglected. Also he worked on the six-year-old Ford pickup as if it were terminally ill, listening to the engine, checking the oil every couple of days, topping off fluid levels, monitoring tire pressure. He let me do the cooking since I was a master at TV dinners, followed by gourmet desserts like Ding-dongs and Twinkies. Truth be known, I think he was eating better despite my unhealthy offerings. In the evening we watched the TV news, any baseball game that we could bring in, and a few corny comedy shows, the older the better. But while the weather remained warm and beautiful, we spent a lot of time on the deck in mostly solitary contemplation.

During one of these grand evening encampments, I muttered about getting a new boat. "Why?" Rolf asked, "You have two perfectly good ones."

"Well the Jonboat is small, and I only use it for decoys and an occasional retrieve during the hunting season. But the bench seats in the fishing boat are too low for both of us. Bad for old joints."

Rolf was immediately defensive. "Don't go changing anything or spending any money on my account."

"It's on my account too." I had undergone lower back disk surgery twice five years ago, and still had nerve pain, spinal complaint, down my right leg. Those low boat benches, with knees in your face and the twisting it took to run the motor, involved more contortions than my vertebrae cared for. Often lately the best part of fishing was getting out of the boat.

"Well if you need it okay, but I'm all right with this boat," Rolf insisted.

He protesteth too much. That right knee was bothering him. I'd catch sight of him rubbing it when he inhabited his own world. My back surgery had caused me to quit jogging and golf. Except for walking, puttering about the cabin and the hunting and fishing, I pampered my back. I had no intention of ending up in some rehab center enduring sing-alongs with old hags.

I told Rolf how the doctor had advised me to limit extended, severe back motions, and he was predictably disdainful of the medical profession. "Ahc, those damn doctors. Don't do this, don't do that. One of these day's he'll tell you to just go croak at the poor farm."

When depressed and wanting some sympathy, our elderly relatives had frequently spoken of the "poor farm" as being their likely destination. It was years before I saw the Ramsey County Farm north of St. Paul with its adjacent home for the elderly. It didn't seem too bad to a kid like me. It would be a hoot to live on a farm. It existed in the days before lavish extended care facilities, when we largely cared for our own at home.

I had a new boat in mind before gimpy Rolf had come along. It was not an insignificant investment. My current rig had cost only about $1,500 ten years ago. A boat with the deeper gunnel, forward controls, real seats and more power was going to cost closer to $15,000.

Days later, out of the blue, Rolf was still contemplating the new boat and bad back discussion when he said, "I thought you had a retriever."

It took me a minute to recycle my thinking. "Yes, I had a great Labrador, Bo, my friend and constant companion. But he developed a tumor last year and I had to . . ."

My emotions surfaced quickly, and I hesitated, getting them under control. My tear threshold had become a narrow thing in recent years. "The vet couldn't cure him, and I couldn't let him suffer."

This long after Bo's passing I still had trouble thinking about him without getting gloomy. In my adult life I had never known a creature more devoted or loving, a bachelor and his shadow. I hadn't cried when Karen left me, but I balled like a baby when Bo died. There were those who thought I might join him. Rolf allowed me to sit in silence for a time and then, almost to himself, he said, "He was loyal."

Some days later he rekindled the conversation: "So you hunt alone now. That must be hard. I never had a retriever, never had any kind of dog, but I know it's a lot easier when an animal can do the water work."

I worried that this line might lead to a renewal of the Bo subject. "Yeah, but now I have you. The first duck we can't wade to this fall, I'll push you in the water, and yell, 'Fetch,'" We both savored the mental image.

Two weeks after Rolf had settled into lake living, there was a check in the mail from the estate sale people for $2,800.

It seemed pretty paltry to me for a lifetime of accumulated furnishings, but everything in his house had been old and worn. Rolf was as pleased as if he had won the lottery. "I never gave it a thought. Figured we were just paying them for junk removal, although I am a finalist for that Publishers Clearing House sweepstakes."

"So is my Uncle Kevin," I responded, "and he died ten years ago."

Rolf held the check for some time and mulled his good fortune. "Found money, my mother would have called it." He had either forgotten about the estate sale or had low expectations. "Now we can get that new boat for you."

"We'll see about that, but first let's go up to the resort and you can buy us a decent meal. I'm getting tired of my own cooking."

Just a mile or so up the lake, where County 35 crossed, defining North and South Ten Mile, was a resort that had been in the same family for nearly 100 years. It was not a "thirty-six-hole-hot-tub" sort of place. You didn't see any dudes in Ralph Lauren shirts with tiny horses embroidered on the pocket and pink sweaters hung over their backs, arms decorously folded in front. This was a fishing camp: a collection of small cabins and house trailers frequented by fishing families who came year after year, like tribes to the Buffalo grazing lands. The most ardent gatherers were those from nearly lakeless Iowa. They worked Ten Mile in shifts, always harvesting. And like starving Armenians, they saved every catch. Nothing went to waste. Even rough fish filled their coolers for future gourmet delights ala-Iowa.

Later generations of the resort ownership had built a steak house, making the place as famous for its beef as Ten Mile Lake was for its fish. Both tourists and locals filled the place on weekends between the fishing opener and the end of duck hunting. It was Rolf's first time there, and he felt a little out of place since I knew a lot of the help and the customers. But each person who saluted me, also made eye contact with Rolf, and after being introduced, put out a hand and greeted him warmly.

As we entered I hailed the proprietor with my standard: "Innkeeper, water for my horses, whiskey for my men!" The resort crew gave me their usual good-natured smiles, tolerant of my elderly tomfoolery.

"The first of my desperados has arrived. Carl, meet Rolf." The proprietor thrust his hand across the bar for Rolf, who was looking slightly embarrassed at my antics.

The fourth generation managers, Carl and Axel, were brothers. The young serving wenches (no wait-person nonsense this far from the big city) came and went but were all locals gals. I called them Chuckles, Bubbles, and Cuddles because I couldn't keep their names straight before they married and moved away.

We had no sooner settled on bar stools to wet our whistles when Ed Lundquist, a burly local deputy sheriff, strode in with his third wife, a young looker. "Are you staying out of trouble?" he asked me, dispensing some police humor.

"Now that I have a warden," I said, introducing Rolf again.

As they moved to their table, Rolf shook his head and muttered, "Three wives." Ed swaggered, she sashayed, buns counter-rotating in tight Capri pants. I explained that he farmed when he wasn't sheriffing, and the curvy Mrs. Lundquist was a real estate agent although an unlikely looking one. I guessed that that gave them multiple incomes.

Chester and Lester Johansen sidled up to the bar on adjoining stools, and I introduced them to Rolf. The phrase "bachelor Norwegian farmers" may have been coined with them in mind. Chester was so rotund that his bib overalls had enough material for a squad tent. Lester was tall and skinny as a telephone pole. Both were in their late sixties or early seventies and, except for their Pioneer Seed Corn caps, as different as dogs and cats. Chester never quit talking and Lester never opened his yap, a little like Rolf only more so. Chester was a happy fellow who enjoyed our company or anyone else's, since his brother had apparently taken a vow of silence. When amused, jolly Chester would laugh with a little, "Tee he," that seemed to emanate from a small inner child. I always chatted with him for a time just to hear that silly laugh. Lester ignored our discourse and kept his focus on the behinds of the waitresses.

Neighbors Paul and Ida Hansen came in, giving me an opportunity for a formal introduction. Paul was a World War II type wearing a 101st Airborne Division reunion cap. Within minutes of his gentle, friendly questioning, it came out that he and Rolf were in the same hell in 1944. Ida, always worrying about my solitary welfare, immediately decided to make a project out of Rolf. "Dear, you look like you haven't been eating well. I'm making up some casseroles for our church social and I'm going to drop by with one for you and Mike"

"God knows I'm doing my best to raise him. What's wrong with tube steaks and baked beans?" I protested.

Rolf, who had lumbered off his stool to give her a courtly bow, was again embarrassed at the attention and could only answer, "Ahc."

"Try the rib eye and the cheesy hash browns," Ida continued undaunted, "that'll put some meat on your bones." They moved on to join a gathering of gray heads at a large table. The women of this group were all dressed up, hair freshly done, and the men (Paul excluded) were mostly in uniforms of colorful golf shirts, white patent leather shoes, and checked pants, easy targets for an air search.

The Hansens were followed by a noisy parade of ladies I had dubbed the Merry Widows. They came babbling past us, accompanied by a haze of perfume and excess makeup. They bore those sort of names that had gone out of style: Gertrude, Opal, Helga, and Mildred. The youngest, Millie, a great looking gal and still a flirt in her mid sixties, slapped me on the back. "How ya doin', Mike?" We had been bridge partners at a church gathering for seniors without purpose.

"I'm still on this side of the sod."

They eyed Rolf, who seemed momentarily stricken that one of the widows might engage him in conversation, but they were immediately ushered to their table.

When Bubbles told us our food was ready, and we finally settled at a booth, I ordered a glass of wine and Rolf another beer. He went after his rib eye like a ravenous dingo, declaring that it was some of the best meat he'd ever tasted.

After returning to the cabin, we settled down for what had become our decadent evening ritual: sauce and cigars on the veranda, a beer for Rolf, a noggin of single-malt sipping Scotch for me.

Gazing once more at nature's twilight pageant, over our particular view of lake and woods, reminded us of the old Hamm's Beer commercials and the accompanying jingle: *"From the Land of sky blue waters, comes the beer refreshing, Hamm's."* Rolf observed that the animated dancing bear in that TV ad resembled Chester Johansen. Then he added, "By Golly, but these *are* friendly people up here."

FIVE

A S OUR SUMMER DAYS ebbed toward fall, we contemplated the joy of the hunt that would be upon us early in October. Rolf had been expressing some guarded concerns about hunting from the Jonboat, because of his knee problem, so I had driven him to the place I leased from a local farmer on Four Mile Lake. It was really gentleman's hunting, just a short walk from the truck to a blind where we mostly did pass shooting. The boat was only a convenience for decoys and retrieving. Once he looked over the ground he felt better about the setup. We hunted between slough and lake on the edge of a soybean field.

This is the edge of resort country where the glacial lakes and old growth forest peter out and cash-crop farming begins in earnest. Before being colonized by immigrant farmers, it had been the edge of the tall grass prairie. My hunting lake was hard by Minnesota's little-known "great divide." From an elevation of just 1,168 feet above sea level, Four Mile corkscrewed west, toward the Red River of the North, ultimately draining into Hudson Bay. Just scant miles to the east, the croplands tilt imperceptibly so that Ten Mile Lake drained into the Minnesota River, thence to the Mississippi and the Gulf of Mexico.

T HE ADVANCE OF FALL HAD US BOTH concerned at the lack of any sale of Rolf's house in the Cities. The real estate agent said it was a good house, well maintained, but in a deteriorating neighborhood. They recommended some modest redecorating. Rolf advised the agent to discount the place liberally in order to sell it, having neither inclination nor funds for any enhancement. "Ahc," he grumbled, "I'll be lucky if I get enough out of that old place to buy a hunting license." I knew he was fussing over sharing living expenses, although his presence cost me virtually nothing. He had repeatedly made reference to pulling his weight. With no sense of the housing market I was unable to reassure him, so it was with some amazement that we soon received a call that the agent had an offer in the $90,000 area. Rolf jumped at it and within four weeks the proceeds less a commission would appear.

"Now we can get that boat," he exalted. Again I slowed him down. We wouldn't be on the lake much longer as the cold winds and falling leaves told us, and I didn't want to appear to be plundering his newfound fortune.

We went to town the next day to set up a savings account for Rolf. Then in a flash of common sense I suggested we see my attorney, Mark Anderson, to get our affairs in order. He urged us lone eagles to have new wills granting each power of attorney for the other. That done we indulged ourselves to a pair of leather recliners, which Rolf insisted on paying for. "They really make your ass smile," I said as we sat in our black leather like a pair of old monarchs observing our realm.

"More like a pair of old farts," Rolf countered.

The next morning I announced that I had a surprise trip for Rolf's enjoyment. "You're taking me to the zoo?" he asked sarcastically.

"No, better than that, I'm taking you to the annual Pioneer Thresherman's show in Dalton." For decades the locals had celebrated the harvest season by an annual display of modern farm equipment alongside ancient farm machinery. It was held at a small county park in Dalton, and although Rolf feigned indifference, the master mechanic was soon in his realm. The great steam engines, some nearly 100 years old and as big as Sherman tanks, chugged and huffed, belching smoke as they lumbered about the grounds.

While I sucked on a beer and watched the strolling girls, Rolf stuck his head right in amongst the pistons, connecting rods, and flywheels to see how things worked, engaging the exhibitors in discussion. The old guys who tended these dinosaurs of early farming were delighted to have someone, anyone, who would display such intense interest in their hobby. And Rolf was homespun enough to fit right in with the farm folk. I thought he might swoon with joy when they staged a tractor pull.

I had to drag him away after several hours as he swore that this was the most fun he had had since, "Damn if I can remember."

In the fleeting beauty of a Minnesota autumn the lake began to reflect the changing season. The chop was frequently from the northwest now and the noisy water bikes and water skiers were gone. So also was the pair of loons who had claimed our side of the lake as their domain. Early one evening, after the sun had set and the sky was turning deep blue, we were privileged to witness a huge flight of migrating coots (mud hens) checking into the lake. Their passage in the dark was rarely seen, but they were the harbingers of the great southern migration of waterfowl on the Mississippi Flyway. During the day they floated about in closely packed flocks that from a distance could resemble a sea serpent. Their daytime flight, if any, began with much furious paddling of feet and beating of wings. This comical churning of the surface rarely got them above an altitude of twelve inches, ending after a short distance in a controlled crash. One cold night, when the ice would begin to inch out from the shallows, in response to some intuitive trumpet call, they would gather unseen in the dark and vanish south to winter in the Gulf of Mexico's coastal marshes.

Rolf indulged himself in a new Remington automatic 12-gauge shotgun and some suitable hunting clothes just before the opener. It was the largest personal expenditure he had made since the money from his home sale. He had kept trying to lavish it on something for me, but except for the recliner I had resisted. "It's not a dowry to spend on me. Besides, I don't need anything," I'd tell him. "Keep it for the old folks home."

"Ahc, to hell with that. I won't go to one of those places where Willard Scott tells some helpless old prune-face that she's ninety-five years young. I'm staying right here with you, Mike, until I kick the bucket."

Heartened by the affirmation that he felt so much at home, I said, "I'll lay you out right here in the parlor, a nice Irish wake. We'll take the ice from off the corpse and put it in the beer. Then," considering his ethnic background added, "for a the finale, a Viking burial on the lake, flaming boat and all."

"By God, Mike, I'd like to be awake for the whole thing."

"I don't know if I can arrange that."

Old people in the twilight of life tend to joke about death, as if humor and feigned indifference might forestall the inevitable.

SIX

THE DUCK OPENER WAS A Saturday near the first of October, and always staged at noon to give the ducks a chance and aggravate the hunters. Ducks don't fly much at mid-day; particularly this opener when the temperature hovered near seventy-five and the wind took a day off. The code of the waterfowl told them to buzz about toward sunset in search of a place to settle, but the Department of Natural Resources limits shooting to 4:00 p.m. for about the first two weeks, in order to give the ducks another break. So noon to four we mostly sat and gazed at swimming ducks, swatted mosquitoes, and realized we had over-dressed.

We assured ourselves that it would be better tomorrow with hunting allowed a half-hour before sunrise. Although we shot a few holes in the sky, nothing really challenged our weaponry. "It doesn't matter," Rolf said. "A day in the boat or in a blind in this country is infinitely better than any day in the big city."

The next morning we were up long before any sensible people and nestled into our pit on the shore of Four Mile Lake as the eastern sky began to awaken. "What are we four miles from?" Rolf asked. I was stumped, had never thought about it. "Are we four miles from Ten Mile?"

"No, we're about two miles southwest as the crow flies. "Damned if I know what we're four miles from or for that matter what it is that's ten miles from Ten Mile Lake."

We were trying to check the time and load our shotguns. I fumbled in the dark and was cursing myself for trying to load a chap stick in my gun when a flock of blue bills thundered over us, diving out of the lavender western sky. They had been in range and passed right over the blind with a whistling of their wings. "Holy cow!" Rolf yelled. "They sounded just like incoming artillery. Scared the hell out of me." Then he chuckled at his reaction and the victory of the ducks.

"They dive out of that dark stuff in the west and come over us about 120 miles an hour, " I noted. "Happens nearly every morning at least once. You just can't see them in time." Neither of us had even gotten our shotguns to our shoulders.

"Still it gave me a thrill just to hear them," Rolf said. "I'll watch west, and you look at the lake." It was a good arrangement because I knew his vision was still keen. He had always been an eagle eye.

"Mark," Rolf soon said, and I wheeled to look into the same dark, opaque limbo where he was concentrating. Nothing.

"Where?" He pointed to a small flock over our nearby slough that was banking in our direction. They were 100 yards off but coming fast with a tail wind. "Lead 'em," I urged.

Whoosh, they were over us. "Bang-bang, bang-bang," our volley of No. 2 shot filled the air, but the black darts continued on, diving toward the lake. "Are we shooting blanks?" Rolf questioned.

"It's the eternal problem with this pass shooting. You have to get way out in front of them, and it's damn hard to discipline yourself to aim and shoot at an empty piece of sky beyond a duck's nose. Well at least we cleared the cobwebs out of the barrels."

We scanned the sky for several more minutes, Rolf focusing on the west, which had produced two flocks, and I squinted into the sun, slowly detaching itself from the trees on the east bank of the lake. It got progressively harder to look east on such a clear day. I had to sneak my focus around the sun. If I allowed my eyes to settle on that great glowing orb for even a second, sun squiggles began to invade my sight and dance around in my vision like orange worms. As the great life-giving body ascended, it cast an even larger reflected light on the water. Both the sun and the reflection were so blinding that I was obliged to raise a hand to screen out the brilliance and search on either side of my paw for movement.

Half an hour went by with nothing else coming over the pass in range and both of us began to feel a chill. "Damn, we left the coffee thermos in the truck."

"I'll get it," Rolf insisted, lumbering from the blind despite my protests; "No, no. You stay here. I'm not useless."

I had warned him to stay on the dirt road because the ground in the surrounding farm field was uneven. The soybeans had been combined, and the soil already plowed and disked. On his return from the car, I heard a grunt and a muffled curse as he approached the blind. He was down on his knees at the edge of the plowing.

"Are you okay?"

A crabby, "Yes, damn it," was the response, making me sorry I had noticed or asked.

"Well, you're scaring the ducks flopping about there in the open. Can I help you?"

"No, damn it," as he used the shotgun to hoist himself, then clambered into the blind muttering, "Damn knee."

"Rolf, you ought to let a doctor look at that. It might be . . ."

He interrupted, "To hell with that! All I need is some of that Viagra." I hesitated, considering whether he was kidding me or getting dim witted. He had a wry way of floating a subject so you were uncertain if he were playing the fool or toying with you.

"You need some iron in your knee not lead in your pencil."

But he seemed to be ignoring me as he stared toward the slough. "Mark, west!" Black silhouettes were rising out of the slough. It was a pair of big greenhead mallards, low and still climbing as they passed over the crop stubble.

Instinctively each of us picked out one nearest to our position. Two shots rang out as one, then both mallards dropped on the bank of the lake. Rolf's was dead and mine was wounded and making for the water. I jumped from the box and down the bank to retrieve the birds.

"There," he said, "we finally got organized."

"Good shot, Rolf. Yours fell dead. Mine is going to take a little neck wringing."

We were pleased with ourselves. "As my dad used to say, 'It shickles the tit out of you when things work out as planned.'"

We examined the two plump young drakes, their iridescent head coloring not yet full, and complimenting each other as if it had been an Olympic event, we took a moment for a celebration. With coffee we sloshed down cookies that Ida Hansen had dropped by with her last hot dish. Suddenly our adrenaline was flowing and the chill was gone.

While we had our heads down, fiddling with the coffee, another flock of blue bills thundered over us and were out of range before we could react. I swore that the ducks seemed to have an instinct about when the hunters weren't paying attention. "Oh, don't let it bother you, Mike. It's been great fun just being out here." Except for that game knee, Rolf was enjoying himself a bit more, his cares fading if not departing.

SEVEN

THE DUCK OPENER HAD BEEN so warm and relatively unproductive that we decided to get back to fishing and add some pike filets to our winter larder. Rolf decided to cast into shore, toward the shallows, for northern pike while I trolled for walleye. I complained that the northerns were bony, but he seemed oblivious to the many fine pin-sized bones that were common to the breed. Besides, he liked the action of tossing a plug to the very edge of a weed bed or a fallen tree, dropping it just short of a disastrous tangle with reeds or branches, and then repetitiously reeling it back to the boat for another try. My trolling was admittedly boring until something hit the bait.

Rolf used a collection of old lures including one that had to have been intended as a gag. It was a block of wood about the size of a fist, chiseled bow and stern to roughly describe a fish. Painted green with some dabs of yellow, it dragged a large three-pronged hook from the tail, and on its nose were two glass eyes covered by a tiny pair of windowless spectacles. Its weight was such that Rolf could have tossed it half way across the lake. With each cast it landed with a satisfying *plunk* that sent up a small waterspout.

"Have you ever caught anything on that brick," I asked disparagingly.

"Caught a muskie on it once, years ago, so don't laugh."

Dumb muskie probably thought it was muskrat.

We patrolled the west edge of Ten Mile roughly opposite the cabin along a wooded island shore. "What's in there?" Rolf asked, nodding toward the woods.

"Nothing as far as I know."

"No homes?"

"No it's an island, well almost an island, connected to the shore by a very narrow causeway that's barely above water. It's a peninsula, maybe a game sanctuary. I'm told that the adjacent farm once kept cattle out there. But there are no homes. The ground is too low-lying. It's just a maze of densely packed trees and undergrowth."

Rolf's seeing-eye lure plopped down just short of a birch that had fallen from the island into the lake.

"If you don't catch a fish with that you might still hit one and knock it senseless," I offered.

Rolf ignored me as he reeled in toward the boat. "If there's no one living on that island, or whatever it is, then why have I seen lights there at night?"

"I don't know, maybe a fisherman taking a pee. I never noticed any lights. When did you see lights?"

"Twice over the past few weeks. Just a brief flash."

"Are you sure it wasn't from a boat fishing along the shore? Like an anchor light?"

"Nope," Rolf insisted. "These flashes were too high to be on the water. It was like a momentary flashlight beam."

I got a strike and was caught up in the contest to land a walleye, so the matter of the mysterious lights in the woods across the lake from the cabin was abandoned. Still that night as we settled back at the cabin for our evening stogies and spirits, I felt obliged to gaze at the wooded island from time to time.

As warm as the day had been, that evening we encountered a slight chill on the deck. It felt good, as the cold along with our cigar smoke limited the mosquitoes. In our customary silence, both of us gazed to the west, an inky amphitheater without a moon and under a cloud cover. If there were lights across the lake in those trees I would see them tonight.

While so absorbed in our after-dinner drinks, smokes and ruminations, we were both suddenly aware of a stealthy presence at the foot of the steps leading up to the deck. "What!" Rolf said, more startled than questioning.

A dark figure materialized on the lower step, as cabin lights behind us reflected in a pair of pupils that showed an iridescent glow. "Shoo," Rolf said at the same instant that I recognized Tina, Hansen's black Labrador.

"No, it's okay. Come, Tina."

A bit reluctantly, having been shooed, Tina approached me, keeping a wary eye on Rolf. "She's a regular visitor. Must be out on one of her evening sniffs." A great black head nestled between my legs, nose in my crotch, for a good scratch, and then Tina plunked herself down next to me, joining in our feckless ritual. She stayed clear of Rolf, who muttered an, "Ahc," for her boldness in having joined us.

Never having owned a dog, Rolf had given no more thought to the canine world than he had to the scheduled return of Haley's comet. I on the other hand, having lived in close harmony with a four-legged being, considered them other races endowed with variable and unique qualities, equal to us dominant savages in some ways and superior in others. They had a sense of smell that was 1,000 percent better than ours and a sense of hearing that was some 700 percent greater.

While ready to accept us as essentially good, dogs seemed to retain judgment and the right to reassess based on the conduct we displayed. They badly wanted to be our friends, to be liked and be a member of our circle. Dogs understood that some people related to them and others did not. They tried to get into the laps of those who displayed affection, even if it was silly baby talk, and instinctively kept their distance from those who shied away from them.

After the loss of my dear Bo I had resolved not to get another dog, partly out of fidelity to him, and partly because I was afraid to lose my heart to another devoted canine that I might outlive. Still, I never missed an opportunity to give Tina a pat and enjoyed the affection she returned.

Tina's house call had lasted only a few minutes when her ears rose. Belatedly we detected the whistle from Paul Hansen as Tina headed down the steps and off into the dark.

"That is one fine dog," I submitted. "I'll invite Paul and Tina for a hunt before the season ends. He has his own places and does a lot of hunting in the Dakotas, but we get together at least once a year. That Lab is a retrieving machine."

EIGHT

I T HAD TURNED BITTER IN EARLY November, and all the sloughs were frozen. Paul Hansen and Tina joined us at Four Mile Lake for what we knew might be the last hunt. We were obliged to break ice in front of the pass to give Tina a clear entry. The ice only went out about twenty feet from shore but was about a quarter-inch thick. Paul and I could break it easily with vertical pressure and then shoved the slabs of ice out toward the lake's center where a west wind would catch them. The lateral strength of such mini icebergs is remarkable. They are like slabs of steel plate, able to cut hip boots or slash a dog's skin.

Exhausted from the exercise, we were just settling down for a breather and a cup of coffee when the first blue bills dropped out of the western haze and plunged toward the lake. Paul and I were preoccupied with pouring or sipping coffee and only Rolf got a fleeting shot at them. One bird fell in the opening we had just created, and Tina was in the lake immediately having catapulted from near Paul's blind.

No command had been necessary. She knew why we were there and instinctively practiced her trade. Still we called encouragement from the shore as she zeroed in on the flailing golden eye.

She came out of the frigid water near Rolf and me, allowed us a moment to honor her retrieve, and then presented it to her master.

There was a solid layer of low scudding clouds this morning, hinting at unwelcome but predictable seasonal moisture. At least we didn't have to fight that low sun. Certainly the northern birds would be on the wing if this weather extended into Canada. As we chatted about that possibility, another two flights zoomed over us, hell bent for the open lake, aided by a strong tailwind. They were flying in the clouds and dropping down as they approached the lake, employing some sort of internal navigation mapping. All we could do was mark them as they passed over and chuckle at our own ineptitude. Tina galloped between the two blinds as if to question whether we were all attending to business.

We had been outside for less than an hour when Rolf began to lumber out of the blind. "I have to go pee."

"Why didn't you go at home?"

"I did, but the coffee goes right through me." He wandered a ways off toward the lakeshore brush and shortly I heard him grumbling with his brand of cussing.

"Now what's wrong?"

"It's so damn cold my Johnson has shriveled. I can't get it out." He had put on all the clothing he owned and was having trouble with the multiple layers.

From the next blind, Paul Hansen called, "Are you guys marking something?"

Tina ran by to check on Rolf. "Shoo, dog."

"No, Rolf's just out there spooking the ducks while trying to locate his pecker," I said. Despite the wind and Rolf's muttering, I detected Paul's laugh. What we don't go through for the joy of waterfowl hunting. If the government forced us to hunt in these conditions, we'd rise up in armed rebellion.

Rolf returned, making chilled sounds to himself. "I can't take the cold anymore. Not since the Ardennes," he said, clambering into the box. He hadn't mentioned it before, but I knew he was referring to the climactic battle of 1944.

The clouds lowered, and when the rain came it was like small beads of birdshot fired by someone in the slough to the west. We tightened our parkas and took turns looking west. Watching east, over the lake was a snap, but looking into that wind-driven sleet got my glasses wet within seconds. Rolf had no such impediment, so he stayed on the west watch. He resembled, I thought, what Leif Erickson must have looked like facing the North Atlantic gales from the hurricane deck of his longship.

Strange as it may seem, this sort of lousy hunters' weather stirs up the waterfowl. Paul called a flock of big birds climbing off the lake into the wind. They labored toward us steadily gaining altitude until reaching extreme range. Still one V of canvasbacks split our blinds and we all fired. One bird fell in the plowing and another set its wings and sailed into the tall rushes bordering the slough. Both Paul and I jumped out to assist in the retrieve while Rolf, with his game knee, marked the angle of the felled cripple.

Tina was on the bird in the plowing quickly. After bringing it to Paul, she ran toward the cattails that surrounded the slough. She vanished into the reed jungle before Paul and I reached it. As we began plowing through the rushes, I took a quick look back to get my bearings. Rolf was standing in the blind and waving me to the right. Within a few steps we were both lost to Rolf and each other in dense cattails taller than our heads. Our boots crunched thin ice, and visibility was limited to what we could see straight down. I could hear Paul calling to Tina from just a few feet away but was uncertain how far his voice carried in the cattail forest with the wind howling overhead.

"Is she with you, Mike?" Paul yelled.

"No. She entered the weeds pretty close to here, but I can't see her, and I don't hear her collar." ID tags on her collar could usually be heard jingling when she was close by. But in this jungle and with the wind, that sound was muted.

Paul began blowing a whistle, and I started calling out as we both edged further into the terrible rushes. By the sound of our voices it was obvious that were no more than twenty feet apart but were totally invisible to each other. The water had now gotten knee deep as we broke through surface ice. I knew Paul had to be worried sick. This sort of ice could hurt Tina if her legs broke through, leaving her in trouble only a few feet away from us.

A single shotgun blast sounded from behind us. "What the hell?" Paul said, in exasperation.

"Rolf wouldn't be shooting over us. Maybe he's trying to signal."

"Well you go see what he wants. I can't leave here without the dog." There was a ring of desperation in Paul's voice.

"You stay there and call to her. I'll follow my tracks back out and look for her as I go." Tina could be out on that slough tracking a wounded duck, or she could have broken through the ice and be hung up. We'd have to thrash our way through that awful cover and find her, no matter how hard or how long.

I backtracked to where I could begin to see through the top of the whipping reeds and make out the ridge along the lake where our blinds were. As I rose, and the cattails lowered, I saw Rolf standing between the blinds waving with both arms. With the wind at my back I couldn't hear what he was saying, but as I focused on him I made out a Lab standing alertly next to him.

After I recovered Paul from the reed jungle and slogged back, we all had a good laugh and rained compliments on Tina. With that great nose of hers she'd found the second duck and did the sensible thing returning to the blind, assuming her master might be there, at hunting headquarters. "That dog's smarter than all of us," Rolf observed. We broke out the coffee and some of Ida's cookies for a mini celebration. Despite the cold, Paul and I were exhausted and dragging, but Tina just shook her coat, spraying little beads of water and ice on us before she enjoyed a treat, then she was ready to go again.

We over-seventy-year-olds were worn, winded and ready to head home, but on the west wind we caught the siren call of Canadian honkers. Normally the Canada goose is very wary and flies above gun range. They read the landscape well and have an innate feel for what altitude is safe from hunters. However, the low clouds and the wind had perhaps given them a false sense of security. What sort of fool humans would be out on a day like this?

They were obviously heading for Four Mile and let down sharply just over the shore north of us, diving and rolling to spill the air from their wings. Then the flock of eight made a wide turn over the lake to the south and began a landing approach into the wind, seeking shelter right in front of our blinds. It was as if they were decoying, but we had no decoys out. "Stay," Paul was repeating to Tina, who sensed our anxiety, heard the yelping of the geese and was in a state of high anxiety.

The three of us arose at the same time and each dropped a goose in the lake. Second shots dispatched the cripples. But they were not in wading distance from the bank, and the offshore wind began to carry them. Tina was on the job immediately, while I legged it for the Jonboat in the back of the truck. I thought it unlikely that she could corral all three without a killing swim.

I dragged the boat from the truck, and got it down the bank, all the while wondering how far the west wind would blow me onto that lake. Before I could don a life jacket, I looked out and saw Tina's head, far from shore, pursuing the body of the last goose. How could I hesitate? She had already retrieved two birds and was forty yards out on a third mission. My God how could she continue these athletic feats? Paul had waded out to the limit of his hip boots, trying to call her back. But as I launched the boat, I knew she was not going to return as long as that downed bird was in sight. This was what she did, her reason for being.

Tina not only had the supreme mission of an endurance dog paddle but the task of keeping the target in sight. A retriever's eyes are only two or three inches above the water, and the increasing chop of waves caused the downed bird to be lost from the dog's line of sight at times. Tina employed that great nose in the pursuit, but the wind, at her back, was no aid.

The flat bottom Jonboat was great for a slough on a calm day. But Four Mile Lake looked like Superior in the fabled gales of November, and I shoved off with some trepidation. If I capsized with the hip boots on, they would be like a Mae West around my legs. The boots would go up as my torso went down. The only way to keep my head up, should such an emergency occur, was to fill the boots. Hip boots full of water might as well be filled with lead. It would be a struggle to walk in shallow water and I'd drown in deep water. But out I went. No time to remove the boots. It was *noblesse oblige* time.

I was not far out, realizing that the wind was already propelling me—I didn't need the oars—when Tina got to the goose, grabbed a mouthful and turned back. I maneuvered so as to overtake her, thinking that I would pull her into the boat, and praying that doing that wouldn't put both of us in the lake. But courageous Tina would have none of it. Lacking my high profile sail area, she passed me, beating her way toward shore, snorting for breath, with twenty pounds of goose in her jaws. As I struggled mightily to turn the boat and follow her, I wondered at just how much punishment the lungs and heart of a two-and-one-half-year-old Lab could take.

51

I could hear Paul and Rolf calling encouragement to Tina as I alternately whacked at the wave tops or flailed the air with my oars. Paul was edging out ever further to meet the dog and relieve her of the burden, shipping water into his hip boots as he and Tina merged. *How about me? How about some cheers for this old fart?* I finally got in the lee of the bank, and stepped out in shallow water. It was easier to drag this tub than to row it against the wind. Paul and Rolf both assisted in getting the boat out of the lake then helped me up the bank. I was sweating despite the cold and breathing like a marathon runner. But there was Tina, shaking the water off her coat and standing proudly over her three geese. She looked at me as much as if to say, *"Why were you taking a boat ride on a day like this?"*

The redoubtable Tina may have been ready for more, but Paul had two boots full of icy water, and we had tested ourselves beyond reason. Starting back home I recalled my father's view of such trying hunts: "It's like hitting yourself on the head with a hammer. It feels so good when you quit."

NINE

A S COLD, EXHAUSTED AND miserable as we had all been from the last hunt of the season, we felt like hunter-gatherers of old when, a week later, we settled at Ida Hansen's table for a great goose banquet.

The Hansens were that unnaturally handsome couple in the retirement community advertisements. He looked like a fifty year-old, tanned beneath a full head of silver hair. Ida was one of those rare women who had retained her girlish figure and avoided the ravages of time. She was a beautiful blonde, turned silver, displayed prominent cheekbones and enchanting green eyes. She was a real babe. But her most marvelous quality was a nearly constant smile that lit up her face. Ida wasn't gushy, just genuinely happy to interact with others. That joyous personality was something totally lacking in the ex-wives of Mike and Rolf.

Paul had smoked the geese and then Ida had worked her magic. The result was beyond bon appetite: smoked goose breasts on a bed of wild rice garnished with bacon bits and water chestnuts and smothered with Ida's special béarnaise sauce. There were biscuits and several side dishes of vegetables, too much.

I had never had a lot of luck cooking goose, so we had readily agreed to let the Hansens do the honors. Geese and ducks can be tender as chickens or gamy as old sweat socks, and mine usually resembled the latter. Lord knows I had tried every sort of marinade scheme, first on myself and then on Rolf, but the dish never came out like Ida's. Regarding my most recent attempt, Rolf commented, "Even the gravy was tough."

"No complaints," I said, "until you've walked a mile in my hip boots."

Paul and Ida were gourmet cooks, aware of my limited kitchen skills, and loved the by-play between us two old geezers. Along with everyone else around Ten-Mile Lake, they regarded us as the odd couple. We admired their home and their gracious company as we gorged ourselves then indulged in an after-dinner drink.

The Hansens possessed a beautiful split-level, four-bedroom house with attached garage about 200 feet south of us. The place had the warmth of a woman's touch that my spare cabin lacked. The only noticeable macho feature was a gun cabinet where antique and working weapons were displayed.

Paul was a retired St. Paul attorney, and Ida had been a schoolteacher before they married and she became a full-time mother. Family photos adorned the walls, and current snapshots plus some crayon art was magnetized to the refrigerator. In summer their place often bustled with their two daughters and several grandchildren.

Knowing that Rolf and I had flunked the life course in family, they thoughtfully steered the conversation in other directions: hunting, fishing, and the joys of lake living, but their kids often entered the conversation quite inadvertently. Paul told a vignette about how a northern pike, thrashing in the bottom of his boat, had tossed a lure into him and sunk the hook through his index finger. He had been faced with running the boat back and docking it with one hand as a seven-year-old grandson looked on in horror at the stream of blood. Paul said, "The landing net, the line, and the fish were all tangled between my legs, and the plug was anchored in my finger. With that northern flopping around, the whole mess was in motion. So I told Joe to get both feet on the damn fish and hold it down. The little guy was a real trooper."

We all chuckled, but Rolf got a far off look about him. He and I would never have such memories. In the silence that followed Rolf changed the subject. "Have you seen the lights across the lake in those woods?" he pointed to the island west of us, alluding to one of his favorite subjects.

"You know, I thought I did once or twice this past summer, very late at night, but Ida never saw them. It was only for a moment."

"See." Rolf gave me a vindicated look.

"But there are no homes there," Ida offered.

"I've fished right up to the neck of land that connects that island with the old farm over there," Paul said. "You'd almost need a swamp buggy to get from shore to the island. So I don't know who would be out there. Probably kids, and I bet the bugs carried them off. Maybe some day Tina and I will go exploring over there."

At the mention of her name, Tina emerged from under the dining room table to a chorus of cheers. "She had as much to do with this dinner as anyone," Ida correctly noted.

After Tina had savored some goose scraps and drained her water dish, she came over and rested her wet muzzle on my leg. "No, Tina," Paul scolded, but I encouraged the contact and gave her a good scratch. She knew I was an easy mark for a little Labrador lovin' and leaned hard against me.

As I gazed into those trusting, brown eyes that I had loved so, and stroked the great head, Tina spoke in Lab, a soft, "Uh, Uh, Uh," from near her Adam's apple.

Paul gave an understanding chuckle, and Rolf said, "Ahc," at such frivolous intercourse between man and beast.

TEN

THIS IS THE COUNTRY WHERE winter arrives dramatically on the back of an Alberta clipper. Blizzard conditions can develop so quickly that the state has installed swinging barrier gates near the freeway ramps to prevent travel by that small minority who never get the message. A wind driven snowstorm on the plains can create a whiteout from which there is no rescue for twenty-four to forty-eight hours.

This clipper had blown for two days, and the temperature had plunged below freezing. It began as the sort of storm that had stranded and killed many hunters in 1940, the Armistice Day Blizzard. From the sanctuary of our comfy cabin, we watched the cold slowly subdue the last of the open water. Even spume blown by the waves had begun to freeze in ribbed, crochet-like rows, as the ice advanced from the shore toward the middle of the lake. Then after two days, the wind died and the night temperature plunged to zero. Under such conditions the water temperature fell below a level where the sun could assert its warmth. Ten Mile Lake was frozen, and winter was here for its four-month engagement. Snow followed for twenty-four hours to a depth of about ten inches with wind-blown drifts much higher.

We turned off the 6:00 p.m. news and were relishing the goose leftovers Ida had forced on us, though we hadn't put up much of a fight. As we settled at the table looking west at the wintry scene, we heard an unseasonable sound—a small engine not unlike an outboard—gaining volume as it neared us. Then we saw a bouncing light.

"What the hell? Is that your famous island light, Rolf?"

He gave me a critical glance, "No, that light is on the lake."

Our common sense told us that it could be neither a boat nor a water bike. Then it registered that we were seeing the season's first snowmobile coming across the lake from the west, skirting the wooded island and angling toward our east shore. It was just crossing the mouth of the bay that formed our south end of Ten Mile.

Rolf and I had no sooner exchanged worried glances that asked, *"How advisable is that?"* than the light suddenly vanished and with it the engine noise. "Jesus, Mary, and Joseph! He's gone through the ice."

I leaped toward my coat and boots, clapping on a hat, and grabbed a flashlight in one well-organized series of moves, although I had never practiced this drill. "Rolf, call the Dalton Township Fire Department."

"My God, be careful," he said."

As I sprinted down the deck steps toward the lake, I could just make out the black hole in the snow-covered lake despite the darkness. I reached the spot where our boats and dock were beached for the winter and pulled a life ring from a power pole near the waters edge. (It had hung there, unused, for years.)

Stepping onto the lake ice with its snow cover seemed perfectly natural. I was just going for a stroll. I heard a faint call for help and began to make out a head at the black hole. For all the victim knew, no one had seen him, nor witnessed his dilemma. I was still near eighty yards away and called out to him, uncertain if he could hear me.

The snow that had accumulated near the shore diminished steadily, blown by wind, and patches of clear ice began to appear ominously dark under my feet. I slowed my pace and shone the flashlight straight down. The ice beneath me was not transparent, and I could only guess at its depth. I knew that there were at least a couple of inches near the shore, but what was it out here? This had been open water just a few days ago. However, the fault in the ice that had consumed the snowmobile was close to where the lake entered the narrow south bay. Probably some current there had kept the ice thinner.

The pleas for help; sounding like a young person, continued, and I called back and waved my light to offer encouragement. But that commodity was evaporating in my own reckoning. I began to see cracks in the ice. Not gaping, open ones but cracks like in a window glass. *God, how deep was it here?* I had fished it often enough and knew, as I progressed, that it was over my head. *What am I doing?* I began to shuffle, trying to spread my weight and search for evolving cracks. I was still a long way from that black hole. *How much line was there on the life ring?* Only about fifteen or twenty feet, not enough to throw it yet.

As I edged forward I tried to think of rescues like this that I had heard about. A ladder! That's what rescue teams use, a ladder to spread the weight and provide a device to extend to the party in the lake. But I couldn't go back to shore now. I shuffled toward the hole, my panic rising. The dim outline of a head and an occasional upraised hand beckoned me. Housman's words rose from my subconscious: *"Yonder is the gate of hell."*

I could see us both being consumed by that black hole. I had rarely been so frightened, even in the service in combat. My mouth was dry but gave off a brassy taste as I slowed and questioned my technique. *Should I be on all fours?* But the plaintive, weakening cries for help kept coming. *How long can he hold out? I can't quit on him.* But I had a life-long dread of falling through ice and not being able to find the hole. Entombed in frigid water beneath the ice. That dream terrified me more than any real-life experience, being shot at or flying in a disabled aircraft.

At about thirty yards, I finally caught a glimpse of him in my light beam. The young man was trying to climb up on the ice, but when both elbows were in sight the ice broke under his weight, putting him back in the water to his neck. I knew that he was in water over his head, and that made it virtually impossible to climb out. A man in a hole needs either a pull from above or something below for leverage. He had neither. All he had was my voice and approaching beam offering any hope of salvation.

Was that a cracking I heard? I stopped dead and examined the ice around me. In the dull glow of my flashlight it was opaque, but I guessed it was thinner than where I had entered the lake. Then I was aware of a rumble behind me. *Dear God its breaking!* But the rumble, like a barrel rolling on the ice, was behind me. I turned gingerly to see what catastrophe was about to envelope me. And to my astonishment beheld Rolf in the Jonboat, seeming to dig his way toward me over the frozen surface.

My first horrified reaction was that he would be the icebreaker that would surely sink me in the lake. But it began to dawn on me that he had done exactly the right thing. The flat bottom boat had no sharp prow or keel. It spread his weight on the ice, and even if he broke through, he would be afloat. Kneeling in the bottom of the boat he worked like a Trojan. He had had the presence of mind to get a crow bar from the garage, and after launching the boat, was picking his way toward me. It was an imperfect means of propulsion, though the boat tending to zigzag away from each thrust. But there was no manual on the subject and he was making progress, albeit agonizingly slow.

I was surprised that I could hear his heavy breathing over the thumping of my own heart, the old dear. As he got closer he said, "Stay where you are, and I'll get you first."

"God bless you, Rolf. I can't move anyway. I'm scared spitless "

Now there were lights on the shore, and flashing reds, near my place. We were not alone. Someone had come to help or at least witness our demise.

Rolf reached me, and I almost wept with relief to ease myself into the Jonboat, although I knew we still had to reach the kid and return to shore. Now I was yelling to the boy that help was close at hand. "Hang on!" He had apparently exhausted himself and was no longer calling out. *God was he dead or just conserving his energy?* Hypothermia would soon be enveloping him in its narcotic embrace.

With the two of us aboard, the boat moved like a road grader. Rolf manned his crow bar and I tried to help with an oar, which he had loaded. The oar skidded on the ice and was about as useful as a buggy whip. Our slow, arduous progress was not unlike that of mountaineers on a sheer rock face.

As we finally approached the hole in the ice we faced a new challenge: How to get the victim in the boat without capsizing it. The flat bottom scow had little freeboard and was inherently unseaworthy. It was designed for one man in shallow water not three in a lake.

We nosed up to the form in the water and I warned him of the danger. There was no acknowledgment, but I saw a slight movement. "Rolf, you had better get in the stern and lean back."

"Okay," I called to the victim, "grab the bow and see if you can pull yourself up part way." I saw his hands come over the square bow, and then he tried to vault up. He got about chest high and, as ice broke under the bow, he fell back, his water-soaked snowmobile suit multiplying his weight. It was a young man, a teenager, I reckoned. I laid out full length on the bottom of the boat with my head at the bow and told him to try again and I would grab him. Seconds stretched into a seemingly interminable wait. "I can't," he whispered, his hands slipping loose from the boat. He was spent.

I lunged over the bow for a piece of him or his clothing and latched onto his parka. "I got him!"

Rolf leaned far back over the stern, again attempting to counter balance the bow.

"Go ahead, Mike, reel him in." If we shipped any appreciable amount of water we would all be in the lake.

With a great cracking of ice and water sloshing over the bow, I dragged the water-logged youngster into the boat. Then we all lay there motionless for a moment, terrified, exhausted, soaked, but afloat.

After several minutes of labored breathing Rolf and I managed to turn the boat around and aim it back toward the cabin, ignoring the boy who lay like deadwood. It was perhaps just 100 yards but looked like a mile, and whatever his condition his salvation now was ashore.

The boat had broken through the ice, and the weight of it with the three of us would not allow us to ramp up on the surface for a slide to shore. So we began smashing at the ice with the crow bar and the oar. We were making ice cubes and measuring our progress in feet when help appeared in the form in an extension ladder with members of the Dalton Volunteer Fire Department. They threw us a line then hauled us up on the ice shelf. With the far end of the line anchored to a tree many willing hands made short work of the final leg and pulled us right up on the shore

The sixteen year-old Haugen kid from Sunrise Drive across the lake was stripped, blanketed, and carried to an ambulance for a ride to town. "Thanks," he managed tearfully over his shoulder. He hadn't the strength to say more.

Refusing offers of help from the firemen, I began stumbling toward the warmth of the cabin, shaking like the last leaf of summer. The adrenaline rush was over and my underwear was soaked from perspiration, my outer wear drenched in lake water from the bottom of the boat. When I glanced about for Rolf he was still half kneeling in the beached boat. "Are you okay?" I asked, turning back.

"I can't seem to get this right leg under me."

Forgetting my discomfort, I bent close to him and put out an arm, "Is it time for that Viking funeral?"

He groaned as I helped him stand. "No, damn you, I'm not done yet. I want another cigar and a beer first."

We huffed and snorted across the lawn toward the cabin steps, waving off the offers of aid from firemen and neighbors. But with one hand on the railing Rolf hesitated at the bottom step and I locked arms with him to urge him forward. "Come on old timer. Remember what my mother used to say, 'No rest for the wicked.'"

ELEVEN

I<small>T WAS LATE AFTERNOON, WITH</small> the fading November sunlight behind us, as we left Fargo en route back to Fergus Falls. Rolf was silent, a study in resignation. The result of the scan indicated that his bad knee would have to be fixed by surgery. "It's bone on bone," was the doctor's verdict. "There is no cartilage, and no medicine to make it any better. It can only get worse. But we can give you a replacement knee."

Prior to the scan the old bullhead had refused painkillers. I had offered Tylenol and the physician had offered him something stronger. But he had insisted he would get better. Will power would prevail. Didn't need to be stuffing chemicals in his belly. He had suffered worse. However, a week after the great ice rescue—kneeling in the bottom of the wet boat on that cold metal had finally done it—he was still just barely able to navigate, and the doctor in Fergus had convinced him that only with a scan at the facility in Fargo could they get a true picture of his right knee and recommend some sort of treatment. Now the final result was in, and despite interminable fussing, we had made an appointment to return to Fargo in early December for the knee replacement operation.

It had been a struggle to get him to agree. It wasn't that he was afraid, but he resisted anything that smacked of aging. And I understood that. It was recognition of the approach of that inevitable process where we began to wear out. Things begin to droop and fail as you limp into your seventies, and some are not repairable. Thanks to modern technology, knee joints seemed to be an exception. But there is a sense of helplessness over these afflictions of the elderly that have the ability to rob us of independence, then dignity.

Rolf also agonized over the cost. Absent any supplemental insurance but less Medicare, it would still be several thousand dollars. "Ahc, the expense. We were saving for that new boat."

"You know that between us there's more than enough for both. That's a silly argument."

Then he wanted to argue medical alternatives. "Maybe we need another opinion. They probably have some sort of a shot for this knee."

"You're like King Canute raging against the tide. We both saw the pictures of your knee. You're riding on the rim. There is no shot for that."

"Who's Canute?"

"Oh, one of your ancestors I'm certain."

Then he switched horses, saying that he didn't want to impose his post-operative care on me. "Oh, hell," I said, "would you leave me to gimp about on one leg? This is something I can do for you. I'm not complaining. It would be a damn sight harder for you if you were alone in the city. Let it happen. It won't be so bad."

It wasn't going to be a picnic for Rolf. Surgery and a two-day stay in Fargo, then back to the Fergus Falls Hospital for a week of rehab, then home with twice a week trips to a therapist. For the likes of me, who had led a reasonably self-centered life, I found myself looking ahead to caring for him. I had enjoyed his company these past months, and thought about how I could adjust things around the house to make it easier for him. The shower stall would need to be rigged with a hose and a stool for sit-down bathing, and he'd need a wedge of some sort under his leg in bed. I'd have to clear the great room of the usual clutter so he could negotiate it with a walker. Instead of dithering about in my monastic existence, I was thinking about living for someone else and felt rather virtuous.

As we turned down Highway 59 leading toward the resort and then home, I tried to cheer him up. "I'll treat you to a slab of prime rib at the steak house."

"The condemned ate a hearty supper," he responded, still grumpy but seemingly resigned.

In fact, I couldn't pay for anything. It was a Friday night, the place was crowded, and it was our first time there since the great ice hole rescue. We entered with my usual greeting to the owner, "Water for my horses, whiskey for my men," and settled at the bar. Various folks treated us to several beers and congrats.

Carl plunked the first two beers on the counter. "It's compliments of the house, and the Haugens said dinner was on them next time you were in." (The Haugen family had already called and visited us, effusive in their thanks. The boy had bounced back to normal after an overnight hospital stay.)

The Merry Widows bought the second round when they spotted us. "Our heroes," Millie gushed as she pressed herself in between us. "We girls want to buy you boys a round. That was a wonderful thing you did." Those clustered about Rolf examined him curiously. Rolf was still a good-looking guy, lean with an athletic build. I, on the other hand, had gained some gravity over the years.

I protested mildly but the beers had already been uncapped and paid for. "Other than rescuing people, what do you boys do for excitement? How would you like to go square dancing with us? A trip to the casino or maybe some bridge." Having planted their spouses of some forty to fifty years, they regarded us as new if not young livestock, suitable for escort duty.

I glanced at Rolf for some comment but he jammed a beer bottle in his face and took an Olympic swig, removing himself from the conversation. I had hoped he might use his pending operation as an excuse, but he abandoned me. "Well, we have our hunting and fishing, Mille," I began to explain, but her mouth was still at full throttle.

"You can't just sit around that cabin all winter. You need some variety. What do you do? Your friend is pretty quiet. Is he shy?" Rolf continued to gulp beer.

"Well we're planning on a new boat, we view the sunsets, and there's our lava lamp." My BS rolled off her like water off a duck.

"Sounds dull as hell. We'll keep trying. We have our ways." She said with a lecherous look and squeezed my arm between her boobs before departing.

"Must have been wearing her Wonder Bra," I muttered. "She almost injured me. Rolf, you could of just jumped into the conversation at any point."

He pulled the cork from his mouth. "You were doing so good I didn't want to cramp your style, and in my weakened condition I didn't want any of those hens assaulting me."

Deputy Sheriff Ed Lundquist and his wife arrived. She strolled past us in her usual self-satisfied, haughty manner, unaware of our newfound renown, but Ed slowed enough to slap our backs. "You boys should leave such dangerous activities to the professionals." He chuckled at his own humor.

"Next time you fall through the ice, we'll remember that."

He swaggered past, unfazed by the intended insult, such was his arrogance.

"Ahc, what a pair," Rolf observed.

We had just settled down to eat when we heard the Johansens' old pickup come chugging and farting into the parking lot. Chester and Lester soon loomed over our booth. "You boys done real good. And me and Lester wanted to buy you a beer. Te-he." Chester plunked a pair of open beers on the table as Lester nodded his agreement and bobbed his Adam's apple. It was as close to conversation as I had ever gotten out of Lester. We thanked them and asked it they wanted to join us, but Chester declined for both saying that they had just gotten there and had some beer drinking to do and didn't want to bother us while we ate. "Te-he."

I finished one beer and raised a fresh one to toast the Johansens for their generosity. "Well, up your lazy liver, boys." Chester te-hed his way to the bar and Lester's Pioneer Seed cap gave us another curt nod before he turned.

"At this rate we'll be in bed early," Rolf said.

"If we don't fall asleep in the booth."

Not a problem. Indeed it was difficult to complete our meal. Ron and Kathy Grugel, who farmed the land where we hunted greeted us next, and there followed more of these kindly, unpretentious people, most we never knew, stopping to pay homage. "I want to shake your hand." "That was a brave thing you fellows did." "Good thing you knew what to do."

We exuded modesty for a time, and then just nodded as we chewed. It was demanding work this hero business, but secretly we both felt like Prom Queens.

TWELVE

THE PRE-OP ROOM IN THE Fargo hospital smelled so strongly of disinfectant and cleaning compounds that it cleared my sinuses and made me cheerily chatty. "Well, I've given my good Type O Irish blood in case you spring a leak on the operating table."

Rolf, quiet and contemplative as usual, failed to see the humor. "If I get your blood I'll probably get roaring drunk on the operating table." From his gurney he gazed at the ceiling so hard that he caused me to look up.

"This will be over before you know it and you'll be good as new. Just imagine, a knee of titanium and plastic. You'll be kicking ass back at Ten Mile in no time."

"I'll be a pain in the ass back at Ten Mile," he countered, as the surgeon entered.

"Good morning, gentlemen. We'll be taking you in to the OR in about forty-five minutes, Mr. Holt." The day before he had briefed us in great detail concerning the procedure and the post-operative exercise and therapy programs. "Any final questions?"

"Have you done this before?" Rolf asked without a hint of humor.

The doctor, a very young man by our standards, didn't hesitate a minute. "Just twice, and so far I'm batting 1,000."

I laughed heartily, but Rolf was stone faced.

"In a minute," the doctor continued, "the anesthetist will be in to give you a sedative and rig you for an IV."

"What he needs is a happy pill," I ventured.

As a pair of orderlies began to wheel him away I groped for the right words that might give him some comfort. "I'll refrain from kissing you. But I'll be here when you come back." Rolf made no response but gave me a glancing look of resignation and raised one hand in a sort of feeble salute.

I must admit that I was concerned for him and selfishly for myself. I no longer had any close friends, just Rolf. And his compass always pointed north, the guy you would want in your foxhole.

Three hours later the surgeon found me and reported that the operation had gone very well. Rolf was in post-op, out like a mummy, and it was suggested that I go home and get some rest.

When I returned the following day I found Rolf sitting in a chair next to his bed. A nurse was just leaving the room and, with a roll of the eyes, threw me a long-suffering glance that said, "You cope with him for a bit."

Rolf had the look of an enraged Tasmanian devil. "That damn doctor sewed my knee to my belly button. I can't get my leg to straighten out."

"They never promised you'd be dancing the jig the day after surgery."

He barely hesitated in his stream of complaints. "The food is lousy, worse than yours, and he stuck a bung in me." The insult regarding my culinary skills was lost in my confusion over the "bung" matter.

"What?"

"I can't take a crap."

The nurse had just returned and offered, "It's normal after all the anesthetic and pain medication. We've given him something for that. Believe me, after our dynamite no one leaves here constipated."

"And another thing," he continued, "I'm not taking any more pain medication. It'll make me loopy."

"Rolf, we know you're no Sissy-Mary, but you need rest in order to recuperate."

My advice was dismissed with a characteristic, "Ahc. Rest, hell. They kept me awake all night, always checking my blood pressure, temperature or some damn thing." He pressed his abdomen, "I'd even settle for a thundering fart."

I knew he would be grouchy as a wounded bear and had brought some diversion, a stack of catalogues from various boat manufacturers. He immediately began to pore over them and, like a child given presents, his misery was cast aside as his mind cycled to boat statistics and paraphernalia.

He was in a slightly better mood the following day. As the nurse had predicted, the dynamite had worked. "Things came out that have been in there for years," he said.

By the next morning he was being bundled up and gurneyed for an ambulance ride to the Fergus Falls hospital where the real therapy would begin.

"You've been expelled from here for acting up," I told him, "so you'd better behave in Fergus."

The next day, as I approached his room, he was on his feet and moving gingerly with cute young therapists on each side of him, and his view had brightened a bit more. "They're making me walk, these nurses. It's a damn nuisance."

"It's been a long time since a woman had you in tow, now it takes two."

He had transferred his complaint about the hospital gowns from Fargo to Fergus Falls. "A hundred years of medical advances and they still make you wear this obscene rig." But he had a bit of appetite back and said the food was better.

Rolf had been an active person in relatively good physical condition, but the constant need to exercise his quadriceps muscles was a source of annoyance. He would admit to no pain but bitched about the routine as if he had other vital matters at hand. However, he improved slightly each day, although asserting that he had probably been crippled for life.

After seven days at the Fergus hospital, he managed to climb into the pickup for the ride home. I pointed out that this very act showed his considerable progress. "I guess," he grudgingly allowed.

We made it up the few steps into the cabin and, although Rolf was not one to indulge in bursts of enthusiasm, it was apparent that he was relieved to have escaped from the hospital. He plopped into his comfy recliner and gave a great sigh.

That evening I cooked walleye, baked potatoes, and sourdough biscuits, one of Rolf's favorite meals. At first he hovered over the dish, head bowed in an almost prayerful attitude. Finally he looked me in the eye with a pained expression. "God, but I'm a miserable old fart. I'm sorry for that crack about your cooking."

"Oh, forget it, " I protested.

"No," he was firm. "I won't forget it. It was a rotten thing to say."

I was anxious to move on, but Rolf still had something in his craw that he was trying to bring up.

"Mike, I'm not one for expressing my emotions . . . one of my many faults. But you are one hell of a good, loyal friend. I'll be forever in your debt. And don't you say anything." He wasn't a hugger but that would have been the moment for it. I got up to get us another beer but kept my silence as ordered.

THIRTEEN

WHILE ROLF WAS CONVALESCING I had been getting organized as the chief caregiver. We had a walker, crutches, support pillow for leg rest and exercise, and I had plumbed a converter into the shower so that he could sit on a plastic chair and bath himself. I let him do as much as he could: bathing and dressing, knowing that he would want the minimum of aid, the maximum of privacy, and recognizing that any exercise was good for him.

As he prepared for the first session in the shower stall, I attempted to help him and noticed a couple of nasty scars, one on his back and another on his right shoulder. These were the result of some old injury not his recent beating.

Then I was needed to assist in getting the sock off his right foot. It was my first view of his bare feet and he lacked several toes. I said nothing but could not help staring. The left foot lacked the little toe and the next one. The right foot had no little toe.

"Frost bite," he said in response to my unasked question. "Happened in the Ardennes."

"From the looks of you I'm surprised you got back. I'd like to hear about it." I knew he would be reluctant to tell of his wartime adventures, so I added, "and I'll tell you my war story."

After supper and Rolf's evening leg lifts, he hauled out the boat catalogs, already dog-eared from his research, and we reviewed the merits of the various models and considered the accouterments: aluminum or fiberglass; power, trolling motors, seating. We were like a couple of kids of yore with a Lionel electric train catalog.

In time we settled down to watch the fire and indulge in our evening ritual: cigars and spirits, Rolf his beer and I my noggin of Oban Scotch.

He nodded toward my glass. "What is that stuff you nip on?"

I held it up to let the fire glow through the amber whiskey. "It's a single malt, sipping whiskey from one of those craggy lochs on the West of Scotland. Smooth as anything I ever tasted. They only make limited quantities. Just enough for me."

After contemplating my choice of whiskey, or my vices, Rolf urged, "Tell me about the Pacific. Any hula gals?" I chuckled. In the entire South Pacific, I had seen few native females and certainly no hula dancers beyond the tourist troupes in Honolulu. He had always implied that my service must have been something of a lark compared to his, and as it turned out, that wasn't far from the truth.

The places I went after my 494th Bomb Group assembled in Hawaii were mostly godforsaken islands in close proximity to the equator. Late in 1944 our first base was on Angaur in the Palau Islands. We flew our four-engined B-24 Liberators to Japanese held targets in the surrounding area and then advanced north to the Philippines and Okinawa. I decided to skip the scenes of airplanes being shot down in flames and the crash landings still etched in my memory, offering the bigger picture.

"We bombed from high altitude, and as far as I knew all we did was rearrange coral, fell palm trees, and kill fish on our early missions. Some of these islands, like Yap, had been by-passed, and the garrisons were isolated and I assume, starving. Still we hit them to keep their runways inoperable and vandalize their vegetable gardens. But then I was a rear gunner . . . guess they put me there so I couldn't shoot down my own plane. So I only saw the targets as we left, went through most of the war backwards."

"Did you shoot your guns," Rolf queried.

"Oh, hell yes. I sprayed my twin .50s at Jap islands as we went past."

"What good could that do?" Rolf continued with a slightly disdainful look.

"It was my contribution to the war effort. Hell, from 10,000 feet you could kill someone by dropping an empty beer bottle."

"But didn't Jap fighters come after you?"

"No, their air defense had been pretty well decimated by Navy carrier air strikes. We never saw a Japanese interceptor until we reached the Northern Philippines. And then one day this lone guy appeared behind six of us. He stayed just out of range and put on an acrobatic show: loops, dives, Immelmans, snap rolls. He could have been the Japanese Speed Holman. I have to say, he had us dazzled with his footwork. Then just as he finished his act a pair of Navy Hellcats swooped out of no place and shot him down. I felt almost sorry for the poor cluck. He was a great stunt flier but a bad warrior."

"Why did you fly so high if there was so little opposition?"

"We flew high enough to avoid their light AA but their heavy AA guns could reach us at most altitudes. Those large caliber guns only fired randomly in the South Pacific islands. I guess they were running low on ammo. As we migrated north, we got lower and bolder, and that damn near got us killed over Japan

"We were over Kyushu in the last month of the war when we were almost downed. Captain Crandall was our pilot and the co-pilot was Lieutenant Touhy. 'Two Landings Touhy' we called him. He was always complaining that he never got to fly the plane. Said he'd only had two landings in four months. I guess Crandall didn't trust him, so if there was any injustice it didn't matter to the rest of the crew.

"Anyway, on our twenty-second mission, the AA was sporadic but around our altitude. Still we ignored it, just black puffs with an orange center a mile this side or that, and mostly behind us. Then as we approached the target, one exploded just ahead of us and to the left of the cockpit. It was the loudest noise I've heard before or since. I thought we had taken a direct hit and started to exit my turret for my parachute. We were still flying but the damage seemed terrible. When I first looked the length of the fuselage I could see daylight streaming through jagged holes and some of the crew was down.

"Crandall had been chopped up by shrapnel. The bombardier, navigator, engineer, and left waist gunner had all been hit to a lesser degree. And Touhy was yelling for some help, and calling for someone to toggle off the bomb load.

"By the time I got forward, others were tending to the wounded. When I got up to the cockpit there was blood everywhere and Touhy was starting a gentle turn back toward Okinawa. Other members of the crew reached the cockpit and helped me get the pilot out of his seat. The flak had turned him into hamburger. 'I need help!' Touhy shouted. 'Sit down there and look for damage out the left side.' I was just a random selection, had never done more than glance at the flight deck. All of our conversation was carried on in a college cheer because the AA burst had blown holes in the cockpit and the wind was howling through.

"I hesitated, looking at the pool of blood and tissue in the pilots seat, its pungent odor hitting my nostrils and momentarily gagging me. 'Sit!' Touhy yelled.

"I clenched my teeth together, strapped myself into the gore and checked the number 1 and 2 engines. The shrapnel had been selective. The engines were still going to beat hell, but a lot of instruments were damaged, radio was out, and we just couldn't consider bailing out or ditching in the ocean with all the wounded. So Touhy headed back toward Okinawa, 300 miles away. Soon someone got the bomb bay doors open and salvoed our load into the ocean.

"Eventually I saw a streamer of smoke from the number 2 engine, next to me, and Touhy directed me to pull the fire extinguisher handle. That put out the fire as he feathered the prop and shut off the engine. The three-engined B-24 was a physical struggle, like driving a runaway team of horses. He had a hell of a battle to keep that old bus from yawing with one engine out, but I helped him hold her on course. We were losing altitude slowly, but he couldn't hold the nose too high for fear of stalling. After what seemed like a month, Okinawa appeared over our nose and we began to let down.

"Touhy's vision was riveted on the runway in the distance. He told me he intended to make a straight-in approach, to hell with the wind direction, and I was supposed to look around for other traffic.

"'There's the flap handle and there's the gear handle,' Touhy roared. 'When I tell you, give me thirty degrees of flaps and then, when I say, lower the landing gear.'

"I was sweating like a pig, but my mouth was dry as the Sahara. It was easy to lose altitude. That B-24 was only too willing to settle with just three engines. But when he gave me the signal to lower flaps it was no dice. They were jammed. So it was going to be a hot landing. Touhy had to use his left hand on the throttles, so he needed me to help with the control column. 'Don't over compensate. Just maintain pressure with me.' Easier said than done. That brute of a Liberator was trying to fall out of the sky, and keeping just enough backpressure on the yoke was cramping my arms and making my shoulders ache.

"Yontan Airfield seemed to be coming toward us at a terrific rate and was lined with aircraft of all types. We would be landing like a runaway locomotive in among all those loads of aviation gas and bombs.

"Just as he flared out a few feet above the airfield I dropped the landing gear. It worked, and we smacked the runway like a dump truck. Touhy killed the throttles, and then with both of us hauling back on the controls and standing on the brakes, we eventually came to a howling halt in a cloud of coral dust, just short of a line of parked aircraft.

"Touhy had made his best landing ever, and it was our last mission. Our pilot died, but the others made it and the war ended two weeks later."

I had been gazing into the fireplace as I related the story, not really seeing the flames—the renowned "thousand yard stare." Rolf remained silent, but the snap of a burning log brought me back to reality. I was perspiring merely from the telling.

As I took a sip of my scotch Rolf asked rhetorically, "How did any of us survive?"

"And why," I asked, "Does the Almighty have some remaining chores for us?"

Rolf shook his head. "Why would He need a broken-down failure like me? I never did have much to offer."

I paused to reflect and considered another shot of Oban. "Well, we're joined at the hip as far as our life achievements go. Maybe the Haugen kid was our reason for living this long. We sure kicked that one through the uprights."

Rolf was looking out the sliding glass doors, beyond the reflection of the fireplace, through the pitch-black darkness, across the frozen lake. "No. There's got to be more. My mother used to say that there was a reason for everything."

"My mom said that too."

"A pair of fine Christian ladies."

FOURTEEN

THE THERAPISTS HAD TOLD ROLF that he couldn't loaf around the house between twice-weekly sessions, not that the patient was so inclined. However, because of the snow and underlying ice it was impossible for him to get outside. So the old soldier clumped up and down the hall and around the great room on his walker, flinging it ahead of him as he exercised his new knee and restored muscle tone.

I busied myself with efforts to beat off the winter, sealing the north and west-facing bedroom windows with clear vinyl. Arctic winter had arrived like a phantom that last week in December causing us to hibernate in our human den. The temperature plunged to twenty below zero, that battery-draining cold common to the North Country. On a clear, cloudless morning, the sun, reflecting off moisture in the air, created fairy dust that settled on every surface with a coating of hoar frost. At night Northern lights kindled a resplendent cosmic display accompanied by a sound like rifle shots—the vertical and horizontal expansion of the lake's mantle causing pressure cracks. The ice symphony was unearthly but heralded a uniquely Minnesota phenomenon. The south end of the lake quickly took on a shantytown look with fishing houses and autos dotting the ice cap.

Huddled near our fireplace, we looked out on this seasonal alteration of our lake view. "Ahc," Rolf fulminated, "Damn fools are crazy. I hate this sort of cold. Can't take it anymore."

There was intensity in Rolf's face as he stared out at the cold, and I sensed that he was conjuring memories of the Battle of the Bulge in December 1944. So after fetching cigars and after dinner drinks, I cautiously probed. "Remember when we were kids and went around with our jackets open in the winter? Bundling up was for sissies. And only the girls wore earmuffs. Once at a hockey game I froze my ears. They swelled up and blistered. I looked like Mickey Mouse for a week. But I was too cool for ear muffs or a cap."

We gazed into the fire as our tendrils of cigar smoke ascended in gothic curls. "Yeah, we were damn fools back then" Rolf offered. "But I grew up in the Army."

"Tell me about it. Were you in on the D-Day invasion?"

As Rolf related the story, his Twenty-eighth Division had missed the historic June 6th landing in Normandy, arriving in July 1945 as reinforcement, but immediately began the drive to flank the German Army. They fought due south then turned east from the Cherbourg Peninsula. His 109th Infantry Regiment was fighting toward the town of Argentan. At a small crossroads village they ran into a determined rearguard. The village was at the apex of a fork in the road and had been leveled by fighter-bombers. Still the Germans held out in the shattered wrecks of buildings. A pair of machine gun crews in the basement of a building at the fork, shooting through narrow, ground level apertures, had an overlapping field of fire that frustrated the advance. Rolf's company had charged the village several times and lost over two dozen men to the entrenched gunners.

"Those machine guns," he recalled "were MG 42s with a rate of fire that was twice any other automatic weapon. Most machine guns went bang-bang-bang. Those MG 42s fired so many rounds at once that it sounded like the roar of a lion, 'Whaaaa.'

And they rarely wounded, they threw out so much lead that they killed. They could cut down a tree or blow down a brick wall." He hesitated, as he invoked a mental image of the scene.

"The road in front of the Germans was littered with debris and our bodies. We were all hunkered down hoping for another air strike or a tank to come help. What we got was an obnoxious major from regimental headquarters who crawled to our vantage point and told the company CO that we had to get moving. The sun was about to set and he said there were no tanks close and no more air support today. But we were exhausted and no one wanted to be next on the casualty list. It was just suicide to rush those guns head-on.

"I was a runner for the company CO, Captain Merriman, and was next to the two officers and the first sergeant, all crouched behind about two feet of brick wall. I was just nineteen and thought they were all old guys. I suppose they weren't any of them more than thirty.

"The German machine guns covered an arc of about 150 degrees, the road and relatively open fields were on both sides. They were just hosing down that road with those guns. And if we tried to flank outside that arc they would fire on us with a 88mm field gun that was in woods several hundred yards behind the village. They may have been getting low on ammo for the 88 or were using it sparingly so that we couldn't pin point its position.

"The major was stating the obvious, that the shortest distance to the village was straight ahead and that the captain had to make another frontal assault up the road. Our CO was reluctant, 'Why not wait for a tank? What's the rush?' 'Because' the major fumed, 'there *is* no God damn tank, and the colonel wants us to take that crossroads today.'

"'Well, be my guest,' snapped the captain, 'and see how many you can get to follow you in a suicide charge.'

"The major didn't make a move, but he began shouting about insubordination and the captain fostering mutiny. When he stopped to take a breath, I chimed in. Don't know what made me do it. Guess I figured I was going to get killed one way or another.

"Captain, I have an idea." All three heads turned to gaze at this dumb PFC.

"I think that if I crawl up behind that wrecked Jeep in the left ditch. I can make a run over the field to the left. I'll be out of the left gun's field of fire pretty quickly, and if I can make it past the right gun's arc they aren't likely to call in 88 fire on a single man. I'll travel light just a .45 and a pair of hand grenades.

"Merriman looked at me as if I had lost my marbles. 'Holt, there's bomb craters and junk of all kinds in that field, not much cover, but lots of obstacles.'

"Yes sir, I've done a visual recon. But I think a lone man might not be as noticeable as a whole platoon. I was a high hurdler. The sun's at my back. Give me a pistol belt and the grenades, and when I get crouched behind that Jeep start some covering fire and show some activity to the right just to divert their attention. Maybe that farm wagon back there can be pushed out by the wagon tongue.

"The major said, 'Who do think you are . . . Napoleon?'

"I ignored him as I began to shed equipment but the captain answered: 'At least he's got a plan, which is something, since all our tanks, artillery, and air force seem to be on vacation.'

"The captain unbuckled his belt and holster and handed it me as the sarge supplied a pair of grenades. The CO gave me a pat on the back, and as I crawled from behind the wall I could hear the sarge yelling instructions to the rest of the company about covering fire. The major looked at me fuming. He was embarrassed and pissed. He was about to say something, to chew me out I think, when the Jerry 88 went '*whump*' and a second later the round came whooshing over our heads in a low trajectory, just like the blue bills, only a lot louder, like a freight train. We were too close to be the target, but the major didn't know that and made like an ostrich. The shell landed well behind us, and while the major was eating dirt I moved out.

"I crawled about twenty feet on my belly to the wreck of the Jeep. It had been turned into scrap iron by the German machine guns that were about fifty yards away. There were dead, including my platoon sergeant, in the road right next to the Jeep. One of the MG 42s had just about cut him in half at the waist, and he was in a pond of blood. The platoon leader was face down about ten feet away.

"I caught my breath and pulled my legs up under me, ready to jump off like you did from sprinters' starting blocks. As I surveyed the field off to the left, sort of picking out my course, I thought of a cartoon I had seen back in England where some Loony Tunes character had said, 'Feet, do your duty.' It got my mind off the dead guys, and I had to postpone my sprint until I could quit chuckling. I took a quick glance back at the wall and waited a few seconds longer. Sure enough, everyone started shooting toward the Germans or just shooting in the air to distract them. Then I got a glimpse of the farm wagon being pushed onto the road.

"As soon as the German gunners started making kindling out of the wagon, I dashed from my position and ran like an elk with a grenade in each hand. My first obstacle was a dead horse, then a couple of trees cut down about two feet from the ground. Next I hurdled a couple of dead Germans and scrambled past a charred piece of field artillery. Then, above the sound of gunfire, I heard some Germans yelling. An MG 42 went 'Whaaa,' and a spurt of bullets tore the ground just behind me. Just as I reached a bomb crater, courtesy of our P-47s, I felt something like a bee sting near my right shoulder blade. As I dove for the hole there was another 'Whaaa,' and the lip of the crater was almost bulldozed over me by machine gun fire.

"I waited there, catching my breath and reaching back to the bee sting. I found some blood but it seemed to be a surface wound. Just a crease, the one you've seen."

Mesmerized by the tale, I spoke for the first time. "You were so fast that a German bullet just nicked your back."

He grinned, "Yeah. If I'd been a half second slower it would have been a cluster of bullets into my rib cage." He brought a hand back to his ribs, still in some wonder at his narrow escape. "And I wouldn't be here to be such a burden to you."

Rolf drained his beer in one swig and thus lubricated, went on: "Occasional bursts of bullets were still digging up the lip of my bomb crater. The Germans were trying to keep me pinned down in case I wasn't dead. But all the shots were to my right. I was pretty sure that I had reached the limit of their arc of fire. So I waited a few minutes more, hoping they'd lose interest in me, or retreat, or take a chow break, or a nap. It worked because they returned their focus to the road and let off a few bursts at the rest of the company.

"Once I'd caught my breath, I came out of the crater on the run toward the machine gun nest. I made it across the left fork of the road and threw myself down by the foundation of the building. The conventional way of assaulting a bunker like this was to climb on top or crawl to the front and lob a grenade through the aperture. But I didn't know if the floor over the basement would give me any protection from the blast, and my amigos were bouncing bullets off the face of the structure with their covering fire. So I decided to look for a back door.

"Remember cellar doors when we were kids? Well sure enough, there was a stairway down into the basement from the outside and its doors had been blown off. Just as I rounded the corner a German came out sensing some threat. I shot him with my pistol before he could turn on me, and then I took a couple of more quick steps and tossed the first grenade through the open door into the basement. I leaned away from the blast against the foundation at the same time that I was pulling the pin on the second grenade.

"It was like poking a stick into a bee hive. There was a lot of cursing and yelling and the Germans began to tumble out. As I began to plug them and worry about what others there might be off to my left, I heard an ungodly wail. It was Captain Merriman and the rest of the company charging up the road, screaming like banshees. God but I was happy to see them. I never saw that major again. I guess he went back to regimental headquarters to tell them he had kicked ass and taken the crossroads."

Rolf went silent for some time, staring off into the fire without focusing, tapping a deep vein in his memory. He had never spoken of this before, but the telling had rekindled the event like opening a dust covered photo album in an attic. Yet his explanation lacked any overarching heroism. He seemed to be the narrator of the event.

As we ambled toward our beds, both exhausted from the tale, I had a lingering question about his missing toes. Where did the frostbite come in? The battle at the French village had been in the heat of August he said. Rolf had yet to reveal the sum of his wartime adventures.

FIFTEEN

THE NEW YEAR BROUGHT an unexpected reprieve from my culinary efforts when Paul and Ida Hansen invited us over for a wild turkey dinner. In preparation for their winter exodus to Florida, they were cleaning out the freezer. It was a bird that Paul had bagged on a hunting trip in South Dakota.

As we stepped in Hansens' door competing aromas made us oh and ah. We not only had wild turkey meat, darker then the farm-raised ones, but Ida laid out a feed as if expecting a thrashing crew: Biscuits, mashed potatoes, green-bean casserole, and rutabagas. Somehow in conversation with the Hansens the subject of rutabagas had come up earlier. Rolf had remembered them as a kid, having seen them at the grocery store, but I didn't have a clue how to prepare the Swedish turnip. I guessed it was the Viking equivalent of the Irish potato. Well dear Ida remembered that conversation and determined to satisfy Rolf's decades long craving. The entire feast was topped off with homemade apple pie.

After dinner I helped Ida clear the table as Rolf and Paul chatted in low tones about how their paths had unknowingly crossed in World War II. Both had been at Bastogne during the Battle of the Bulge in December 1944.

Ida made short work of the dishes, and after giving Tina some meat scraps, we all rallied in their great room over coffee. However, Ida couldn't stay still for long as she felt obliged to Tupper Ware a mass of leftover vittles for us to take along.

It did no good to protest as they were leaving and the food would "just go to waste."

Tina was nuzzling me for some post dinner attention when Paul mentioned that they would leave her at a boarding kennel in the Cities. "No" I said. "Won't she be with one of your daughters?" They explained that one lived in a non-pet town house development and the other was on the verge of a move.

"You can't put Tina in a kennel," I impudently blurted. "She's family."

"We don't have a choice, Mike," Paul said. "Our part of Florida shoreline is anti-dog, and she can't stay with the girls. It's a very nice kennel. She'll be fine."

It was none of my damn business, but I had a soft spot for Labs and this one, who was busy loving me up, knew my weakness. "We could take her," I heard myself saying as I glanced at Rolf.

"What?" he said, with a surprised look. Rolf was not a dog person.

"Well, I didn't kennel you, and you were a hell of a lot more trouble than Tina will be."

I got the expected, "Ahc!" Paul and Ida stifled their amusement and argued that it would be an unreasonable inconvenience. But I responded that I had not had a dog for years, had nothing better to do for a couple of months and, "It would be a nice change from taking care of old goats. Rolf had to grin at that.

Paul and Ida gave each other questioning glances then a, "What-the-hell," shrug.

"I hope it's all right with you," I said to Rolf as we climbed in the truck.

"It's your house," he said, a bit pissed, I thought.

"Don't be like that. It's your home too."

"Well I have never lived with an animal, so I don't know about such things."

"She won't be any trouble to you, and you might be surprised at how much joy she can dispense." He said nothing more. And in the silence I felt obliged to support Tina's cause. "And you can't regard her as you would a cow. Dogs have personality, some more than others. Tina has a lot. She can reason and express affection and," I thought this might cinch my case, "like her breed, she's loyal."

So two days later Tina was dropped off with her substantial belongings: bed, dishes, dog food, Milk Bone treats, various chewers, retrieving dummies, and a pair of well gnawed marrow bones.

She seemed as excited as a kid arriving at camp. While Paul reviewed her feeding routine she bustled about the cabin inhaling the new scents, exercising her curiosity. When he was ready to go, Paul called her over and gave her a final love. She buried her head against him like a bookend, returning the affection. Unbeknownst to any of us, it would be their last time together.

As the door closed and he vanished, Tina acted a bit confused but was diverted by finding me on the floor offering a Milk Bone, a belly rub, and some reassuring chatter.

Rolf watched somewhat disapprovingly, "Ahc! Do you think she understands any of that malarkey?"

"She understands the tone of my voice and that I'm expressing friendliness." Tina leaned against me as she had done with Paul a few minutes earlier. "And she's staying clear of you because she understands that you're not a dog person. At least not yet."

"And she sleeps in here?"

"Sure, she's a cold-weather dog but not a polar bear. I'll put her mattress in a corner of my bedroom right where Bo used to sleep."

"What about going to the john? Do we leave the lid down?"

"No, she's house trained. She'll go to the door or fuss at me when she has to do number one or two. She won't bother you unless you want her to." As I talked I continued to give Tina a thorough scratch, and she reached out with her long black snout and gave me a chin nuzzle along with a, "Uh-uh."

"She'll hunt and fish with us or just lay here enjoying the fire or the sunset. Look at her this way, a woman is just a woman but a good dog is a buddy."

So it was Tina, Rolf, and I for the foreseeable future.

Rolf seemed mildly annoyed with her presence, but for me, she was a great source of pleasure. Just looking at her made me smile: The broad head, velvet ears, noble muzzle, seal-like coat so thick that its angles reflected any ambient light. And although she seemed a bit confused in the first few hours—*This was fun. Can I go home now?*—She stayed near me and began to sense that I was her squire. When I let her out in the bitter cold I went along to make sure that she didn't stray back to Hansens' and to assure that she didn't wander so far that her paws froze. Ice in the webbing of a Lab's pads tended to freeze in deep sub-zero cold.

That first night Tina settled in front of the fireplace and rolled on her back with all fours in the air. I chuckled and Rolf ahced. Tina apparently thought that she was pretty cute and wagged her tail. Harder to do, I would imagine, than wagging while upright. That night when I settled into bed, she checked on me, chin on the bed, then at my command, "Settle down, Tina," she dutifully curled up on her own mattress right near me. Whatever she thought of us old codgers and her new home, she seemed to have resolved matters in her own mind. She was content and I was quietly thrilled, peeking at her long after she had succumbed to sleep.

Awaking near 6:00 a.m. in the winter darkness I could discern a pair of Labrador eyes staring at me intently from about eight inches. *"Are you still my go-to guy?"*

We both had to pee. I let Tina out and cinched up my bladder muscles as I accompanied her. She dashed to an appropriate location in the snow while I danced from one foot to another, freezing in slippers, pajamas, and overcoat. It had warmed to about ten degrees overnight, but an east wind made it astonishingly cold. "Colder than a well digger's butt," we used to say as kids. And why did we say it? None of us knew a well digger, but it was one of our earliest naughty words and made nine-year-olds feel like guys.

Tina scampered in and stood guard at the bathroom door while I had my turn. I dressed and set about making breakfast, pancakes and sausages, hoping to inveigle Rolf into a better mood. The dish would have been superior at the Dalton Cafe where we frequently had breakfast, but it was too damn cold and Rolf was still hard put to navigate over ice.

He caught the scent of brewing coffee and came ambling down the hall with his walker. Tina, who was lying near me in the kitchen, swished a greeting with her tail, but stayed in place. She was displaying friendly but subservient vibes.

Ignoring the dog, Rolf asked about the weather.

"The cloud cover and the east wind tell me we're in for something," I said, snapping on the TV.

We were just in time for the Fargo news, and there was the weatherman centered in the screen. "Look at the damn fool in the middle of the map flapping his arms like a seal."

The weather guys had become one of our pet peeves. "We can read a map!" Rolf fulminated toward the TV. "Get out of the way and let us see it." He took a swig of coffee as the news of a possible blizzard was dramatized for all it was worth.

"There ought to be a rule that those meteorologists have to stand off screen and use a pointer," I offered, thinking that he would brighten if I were supportive.

"And if they show their faces," Rolf proposed, "they get shot."

"Well that might be a bit harsh, blood all over the map, but perhaps someone off-camera could crack 'em with a polo mallet."

Rolf's attitude improved a bit at the thought. "By golly I'd volunteer for that job."

We had received little snow during the past week of sub-zero temperatures. "Too cold to snow," was the saying around here. But now the thermometer was rising and the wind had swung around 180 degrees, and snow was forecast, lots of it.

Even in the most rotten weather, I took Tina out frequently for dummy retrieving of which she never tired. I had always puzzled at how a Labrador could hold an icy hunk of plastic or canvas in its mouth without the tongue sticking like a kid's tongue on a schoolyard pipe. But that never happened. Tina quickly learned that I was the play lady for games and kept trying to induce me outside. Cold as it was, the exercise was good for both of us. Needless to say, Rolf thought we were daft for all the cold-weather frolicking. He continued his exercise routine about the house, shooshing Tina out of his way so often that she took to settling under the dining room table when she saw him coming.

Rolf was due in town for a therapy session, and I questioned if we should go. "Ahc!" he scoffed. "We'll get in there and back before there's any accumulation. Can't be afraid of a little snow. Those TV people are always trying to scare the hell out of the old folks."

"Good thing we aren't old folks," I agreed as I handed him a plate of food.

Having been cheered at the prospect of shooting weathermen and defying the elements, Rolf gave me a half smile. "Thanks for the flap jacks and sausage, Mike."

Tina swished her tail on the floor. Smelled good to her.

Later, as I helped Rolf into the truck, he asked, "What about the dog?"

"She'll come with us." I whistled for Tina and she bounded into the cab.

"What?" Rolf said, aggravated. "Doesn't she ride in the back?"

"No. She's not a duck boat or a load of wood. It's too cold back there, and the wind is bad for a dog's nose. Sit, Tina."

She sat between us looking out over the hood, anxious to be off on whatever adventure was pending. Rolf looked disapprovingly as Tina whacked both of us with her tail. I put an arm around her rear and scooted her over closer to me while Rolf let out a perplexed sigh.

On the trip into Fergus Falls Tina viewed the roadside sights as if she knew where she was going. After dropping Rolf at the hospital I parked the truck and saw him into the rehab center, then went to the grocery store for supplies. When we returned he was waiting in the lobby with a triumphant look, brandishing a cane. He had done so well that they had traded him a cane for his walker.

As he climbed into the cab, Tina was all a twitter and almost gave him a slobbery facial before an "Ahc," drove her back. Again I pulled her rump over next to mine and we started back. None-to-soon. The snow had only just begun but by the time we reached I-94 it was slanting down in near horizontal torrents. The blizzard they had been predicting was suddenly upon us with near whiteout conditions.

I was gripping the wheel tightly, leaning forward better to see, as if that could make any possible difference. As I plodded forward at a modest fifty to sixty miles per hour, other drivers including truckers, were roaring past me like they were on tracks, indifferent to the potential for collision and adding to the blinding maelstrom. The white stripe near the right shoulder was suddenly a vital navigation aid. After being buffeted by another passing semi I glanced briefly at my companions. Rolf shot me a nervous look, but Tina was scouting into the white wilderness, happy as a lark. The tires of the heavy freeway traffic would keep it from icing for a time, but the howling, snow-driven winds created a danger. "I'm going to get off of here at Highway 59. Too damn busy."

Indeed there was little traffic on 59, locals who drove carefully and had their lights on, but the volume of falling snow was already filling the cracks and pores of the asphalt. Even with four-wheel drive I sensed that the movement of the truck was like stocking feet on a waxed dance floor. Easing off to about forty miles per hour, I strained to keep on my side of the road and almost missed the intersection for our crossroads, County 35, Rolf's Viking Trail. Already several signs at this intersection were coated white. A few more minutes, and we eased past the resort and turned on our Bankers Drive. I released my white-knuckled grip on the wheel. With trees and buildings to break the wind, we could now make out landmarks and felt our way home.

We both sighed as we eased into the garage. Rolf worked himself out of the truck and into the house, waving off any assistance. He had needed some with the walker but felt a new sense of independence with the cane. He would have had a tough time menacing me with the walker but made some defiant gestures with the cane. "No, no. I can do it." So I busied myself with the groceries while Tina, free of her long confinement in the truck, did figure eights around the yard enjoying the powdery new-fallen snow.

SIXTEEN

THIS WAS NOT YOUR STANDARD "I'll be home for Christmas" snowfall. It was a howling, malevolent beast that could trap and kill the unwary and would isolate local farms and homes for a day or two. The Highway Department announced that the blizzard gates would be closing to travelers on I-94. Now we would be isolated in our bunker for a time. It reinforced my long-held view that winter here on the edge of the plains resembled trench warfare, boring periods spiced by violent intervals.

The opaque curtain of snow became so thick that even the nearby trees were only ill-defined shadows. And as darkness fell, everything around us vanished. With the cabin dark except for the glow cast by the fire, we turned on the outside floodlights to gauge the intensity of the storm. We might have been the only ship afloat on this sea of snow, bow into the maw of the blizzard.

Whenever there was an intense wind-chill factor, the cabin became harder for the propane furnace to heat. I hauled in extra wood and stoked the fire so well that Tina got too hot and moved from the hearthstone. We bundled into sweaters and indulged in our after-dinner spirits to stimulate our circulation, although we never really needed an excuse. Rolf was in a reflective mood, looking out the window yet not focusing on the storm. Did he want a beer, I asked, or something stronger, hoisting the Oban. "It puts a pleasant warmth in your gullet," I assured him, being an expert on such matters.

"No thanks. The beer will be fine." And for some minutes he continued his contemplation of something seemingly beyond the swirling storm.

"I've had cognac in the past, quite a bit of it," Rolf finally said. "It was great for warding off the cold. Or maybe it just got us happy enough so we didn't give a damn. But I could never afford it back home," he finally volunteered, without diverting his attention from outside. His expression did not reflect the enjoyment of a fine brandy but rather a long-remembered agony.

I sensed that he was only partially with me in the present moment, so after settling with my scotch I ventured, "Tell me about it."

In December 1944, as he explained it, Allied forces had driven the German Army back to its own borders, and there the Allies hesitated to rest and resupply. It was mistakenly believed that the Germans were whipped, and the next push would see their collapse. Rolf's 109th Infantry Regiment was dug in astride the Luxembourg-Belgian border in the Ardennes Forest. Having been in continuous contact with the enemy for weeks, they were anticipating relief by one of the other regiments in the Twenty-eighth Division. Until that time they formed a thinly stretched line facing the enemy to the east.

As Rolf related the story, his squad's position overlooked a stream and a stone bridge that crossed into German held territory. On December 15th his unit was in foxholes guarding the rode that led to the bridge. Rolf commanded a crew of three manning a fifty-caliber machine gun that covered the stream crossing. Riflemen were dug in around them. They had hacked their way into the earth then felled trees to provide frontal and overhead protection.

"Considering that we were camping out in winter in the snow, we had really made our bunker into a comparatively cozy nest. We had a pup tent canvas to keep us dry and a wood fire with plenty of fuel. For guys who had been on the move for many days, it wasn't bad. Our vehicles were just behind us, around a dogleg in the road, and a couple of guys back there were cooking up some hot food. It was slop but hot slop. And we had a few bottles of liberated booze that had replaced the water in our canteens. Of course that was against regulations, but water would freeze in the canteen, and if we felt the need for water we just melted some snow in a canteen cup over the fire. The brandy warmed us. Hell, it numbed our brains so we didn't care so much about the cold.

"The forest was so thick on the other side of the stream that we couldn't see anything. There was no sign of Germans and no movement. We figured they were whipped and finding refuge in cities behind the forest: Schnapps, fires, baths, and frauleins.

"But those devils were sneaking up on us quiet as a bunch of church mice. The heavy forest hid them and the wind masked the sound of their tanks. Early on the morning of the 16th of December we heard engine sounds and a swarm of Germans, led by a half-track, started across the bridge. We could hear other engines revving in the woods over there.

"I concentrated my .50 on that half-track and stopped it about mid point on the bridge. Then we went after the supporting infantry. We dropped a lot of them, but they kept on coming. Random shots were hitting our little fort, digging into the logs but we were relatively safe from small arms. I wasn't worried. Then I saw a big muzzle flash in the trees across the river. I don't know what it was, tank or self-propelled artillery. Its first round sailed over us and exploded behind us past out trucks. But I knew it was just a matter of time, and our little 'Lincoln Log' fort would be firewood.

"There was a split second between the next muzzle flash and the shell hitting the ground just below our bunker."

Rolf hesitated, took a drink of beer, shaking his head as he tried to conjure up that scene.

"I came to eight or nine hours later. Despite the ringing in my ears I could hear German vehicles going by. So I knew I wasn't in heaven, but I was close to hell. So I stayed still. It wasn't hard. I had been buried underneath dead bodies, dirt, timber, and that damn machine gun. The German round had demolished our fort, and thrown the .50 caliber gun on top of me. I had the grand daddy of all headaches, a knot on my forehead—my helmet was dented by the gun—both ears were bleeding, and I had a few other nicks and cuts. But for some reason—only God knows—I was alive and the other two were dead.

"When the sound of traffic died I started to worm my way out of the grave. I scrounged whatever I could. I took a helmet and another coat from one of the dead boys. All my spare gear had been in one of our trucks. And I knew they were long gone.

"Then I began to walk—stagger—in the direction that I thought was due west, angling away from the road and staying in the trees. It had started to snow hard, I was getting cold. Soon it was dark. I hadn't gone far but tromping through the snow soon exhausted me and I lay down. Hell, I fell down. Crawled under a pine and burrowed into the snow and cut a few branches for cover. Snow insulates to a degree. With a few nips from my canteen, I slept, although I knew that in a deep sleep I could freeze.

"When I next woke it was early in the morning, still snowing, and I was stiff as hell. But I knew I had to move and find shelter or die right there. I polished off the last of my brandy and continued west by dead reckoning. I could hear the rumble of artillery far ahead of me and knew that the battle was still going on but couldn't figure out who was winning. That I was behind the Germans seemed pretty certain.

"I walked through that day, or did what passed for walking. Mostly I stumbled and rested every half hour or so. The exertion of walking kept me fairly warm, but I never left the forest, knowing I was safe from observation. A German sniper wasn't going to pick me off in these woods. The snow continued, and I was increasingly aware that there was no sound of aircraft overhead. That was not encouraging, if weather was too bad for our tactical air to play a role.

"As darkness settled in, I was starting to look for another likely burrow, although I was pretty certain it would be my final resting place. I was so cold that I could no longer feel my feet. It was like walking on stilts. Then I stumbled over a pile of snow that turned out to be a stone fence. And as I lay there resting I realized that I was in a very narrow path. It was only about ten feet wide, stonewalls on both sides, and snow covered with no tracks. Still, it was the first sign of civilization I had seen.

"It seemed to run in a north-south direction. South might bring me to the highway and the Germans, so I started north hoping it led to some sort of crude shelter. I stumbled along and was about to give up when I got a whiff of wood smoke. That kept me going, although it was dark and I could only see a few feet ahead in the heavy snow. Then there was a dim light visible ahead. It came and went as I staggered along as if it were a candle showing through a crack in some curtains. As I moved closer, a large house materialized along with other dark shapes of nearby farm buildings. The road seemed to end here.

"There were no military vehicles about so I went to what looked like a front door and knocked. I was ready to make the best of it if Adolph Hitler had opened the door. But it was a small, frightened old man who peeked out at me like I was an apparition. He shouted something and slammed the door. I was torn between drawing my pistol and crying. But I was too wasted even to fight the old man and took a couple of halting steps toward the farm buildings when the door reopened. A handsome, middle-aged woman with a lantern stood there, examining me. The old man and an old lady cowered behind her.

"The old people gasped and the woman looked at me as you would a wounded animal. 'American.' I said, not recognizing my own voice. She cast a quick glance around me to see if there might be others then handed the lantern behind her to the man and reached out for me.

"Come in," she said in English.

"She ushered me down a hall, calling instructions to the old couple in French or Belgian and led me toward a fireplace. The man pushed a large chair toward the hearth. She led me like a child, and as we passed a mirror I was shocked to see the ghoul who looked back. Both my eyes were blackened and dried blood ran down from my ears and there was a cut over my right eye. I had a nasty bruise on my forehead above my nose with a bump the size of half an egg. All this was barely camouflaged by grime and a week's growth of frosty beard. God but I was a sight. I looked and felt three days older than dirt.

"I was too exhausted to do anything for myself but to sit by the fire. So this marvelous lady began tending to me like I was a child—taking off my helmet, unbuttoning my coat, offering me a glass of cognac. Good old brandy.

"She spoke perfect English with the slightest accent, and while quizzing me she was directing the elderly couple to fetch various things. After a couple of shots of brandy I gathered a little strength and began to protest that the Germans might appear, and if they would just get me to their barn

100

I would hide there. She would not hear of it and continued ministering to me, dabbing at wounds and trying to ease my gloves and boots off. She was gentle as my mother would have been, understanding that I might have frozen limbs.

"The old ones called her 'Madame' and I asked her name. It was Marie de la Martinere. It sounded like Martin with a 'year' for a tail. Her husband was a colonel in the French Army and had visited her a month ago. They'd had three sons, one of them dead, serving with Free French forces.

"I continued to worry about their fate if the Germans came, but she scoffed at the thought, saying that they were too far off the beaten track for the 'Boche' to bother. As fast as she stripped me of equipment or clothing, the old guy hid it some-place. It seemed to be a huge place with a lot of rooms. A chateau they called it. The old lady soon brought me a bowl of soup, then some bread, cheese, and wine. I wanted more to eat but Madame cautioned against too much at once.

"Then she led me to another room where the old man had filled a bathtub for me, and to my astonishment this grand lady began to undress me. I protested but she said, 'I have raised three boys, and you will need help.' True, she was old enough to be my mother, and I was too tired to argue, and the wine and brandy had begun to work on me. She was right. My socks had adhered to my feet. She cut them away and skin came with the socks. My feet looked like they were dead. Then she treated cuts on my face and right shoulder. She left and the old man helped me into the tub. I must have smelled like a goat. God but that bath was soothing. Then, as if that wasn't enough, she reentered with another cognac and a cigar. The stogie was a bit stale, but I couldn't have enjoyed it more. The old man stayed next to me muttering occasionally in French—spoke no English—but he too was being very considerate. Waiting on me like I was royalty. I felt like the guy who fell in the outhouse and came up with a new suit of close on, smelling like a rose. Their kindness was just overwhelming.

"She returned with some under things. And after the old guy had helped dry me, she bandaged my feet and I was put to bed: a real bed. I hadn't been in one in months. Mike, I slept for twenty-four hours. And when I woke they started again with this flood of kindness: food, drink, some sort of ointment for my feet and hands.

"I was nervous about being there and compromising their safety, but Madame scoffed: 'Either the Boche are in Paris or on the way back to Germany.'

"It didn't matter. I was barely able to navigate on my newly thawed feet. And since it was still snowing, I settled in for more rest and royal treatment. She was such an elegant, cultured lady and treated me with such compassion. I suppose she was thinking of her own men.

"After four more days in the chateau, I was growing more nervous that the Germans might appear and harm these folks for sheltering me. And I figured the line between my being overrun and being AWOL was getting thin.

"She furnished me with several layers of her sons' clothing to wear under my uniform—which had been cleaned—and I bundled up in my coats and helmet. Then with a canteen of cognac I was off. She wept as I left and hugged me, as did the old folks. And a couple of days later I made it through German lines into the Bastogne perimeter. The medics there were swamped with wounded. Told me I was one of the lucky ones. Later, at a hospital in the rear they cut off three frozen toes."

Rolf's tale of the Battle of the Bulge left him downcast and me bone weary from merely hearing of his ordeal. Again, he had survived against terrible odds. After a long silence he said, "I always swore that I would go back or at least write

Madame Martinere," he said. "But like so many things . . ." I nodded in silent agreement. It was the same with me.

After several moments of contemplation I finally broke the silence: "So were you sent home then?"

"I could have gone. Twice wounded. I was in a rear area hospital in France for almost three months. Mostly getting my feet back in shape. And I was about to be returned to the States when my old company commander paid me a visit. He had been promoted to major and was on the regimental staff. He brought orders promoting me to staff sergeant and a request that I return to the outfit. They had suffered so many losses and the ranks were full of fresh troops. They were badly in need of veterans. I could have refused, but what the hell, I agreed to go back. So for the last two months of the war and three more after that I was in Germany. And when they ordered the entire division shipped home, it was too late for me to go to Belgium. I never got to thank Madame Martinere and arrived home too late to see my father."

In the dwindling firelight, our reflections in the sliding glass doors were of two gray eagles, crows feet etched about our eyes, pondering where our youth had gone, and contemplating the words we had not spoken, the paths not taken.

SEVENTEEN

WE SETTLED IN TO ENDURE the worst of Minnesota's winter, the short dark days of deep cold and often-bitter wind that seem endless January through February.

Tina and I ventured forth to exercise and to relieve the dog. She was thrilled at each indication of an outing, wagging her tail knowingly as I pulled on my heavy gear, but my blood was thinning and I was getting weary of the frigid days. Rolf stayed inside diligently performing his trek about the cabin, like a man on a treadmill. He did begin to worry about the dog's paws in the cold, which I took as a sign that he was warming to her. His own paws were bothered by the cold—a product of his Ardennes Forest adventure—even though he stayed inside in socks and slippers. At times his seven toes would turn white, his feet almost blue and he would look out at the ice fishermen on the lake and mutter, "Damn fools."

Our condition reminded me of a piece of western art that I had once admired: it pictured a gaunt steer, up to its belly in snow, and was titled, "Waiting for a Chinook Wind." That was us. We were waiting for a warm wind to shove the jet stream back north and banish the arctic air back to Canada.

So with little else to do, we read or watched television and grumbled. I had gotten some videos of old Carol Burnett Shows, which we both enjoyed, replaying the episodes with Harvey Korman and Tim Conway. Viewing Tim's shuffling "old-timer" routine Rolf said, "He reminds me of you." And we routinely watched the broadcast news, although we both talked to the TV set. About the thousandth time that I heard them say, "Call us when you see news happening," It got my goat.

"Shit happens," I fulminated at the deaf tube. "News *occurs!*"

Rolf turned and looked at me like I was losing my marbles, and Tina ducked under the dining room table. "Mike, we can't have the zoo keeper going off the deep end. We need you." He was including Tina in the plea. Another good sign that he was accepting her.

"I know. It's just this long winter."

"Well, you can't have a heart attack, or they'll try to shove me in a nursing home." He got a determined look on his face, like he was envisioning such a dread outcome, the wasted bodies, the hopelessness. "I'll be damned if I go there."

"Not my idea of a final picnic either. Let's make a pact. Whichever one of us gets so decrepit that he's ready for the home, the other one takes him out to the pass on Four Mile and we have a fatal hunting accident."

Rolf seemed to give the daffy scheme serious thought. "You know you're not the best shot I've ever seen. So if I'm the one who's selected for departure, for God sake don't wing me."

"Yeah," I said, chuckling at the prospect, "it would really pain me if I had to wring your neck." Rolf laughed so hard that tears ran down his face. And Tina came out from under the table to see what all the good humor was about.

It is said that old age is a state of mind. Neither of us was ready to admit that we were in the twilight of our time. Yet deep down we knew that life as we now enjoyed it had an inescapable terminal point. Reason can often linger while the ability to function declines. When the accumulation of age starts to close the circle from infancy to dotage it is alarming and depressing at how quickly the simple tasks—preparing food, bathing, moving about—can suddenly slip from our grasp. It is a process that signals the possible onset of something often worse than death, dependence and its dread companion dementia.

W ITHIN THE SHROUD OF FEBRUARY our fecklessness reached a new crescendo: cussing the TV, making meals, and exercising Tina were our only remotely worthy exertions. Wallowing in this sedentary mode we also napped a lot. Not that we planned on it, drowsy just occurs to those of us long in the tooth and lacking purpose.

Finally, we decided to stir our stumps and began to restudy the dog-eared boat catalogs, drawing up a wish list of necessary requirements. A beer cooler-live box was our number #1, "can't-do-without" boating accessory. Comfortable seats were next. We had our priorities straight. Once our planning had reached a level comparable to that achieved in the Normandy invasion, we picked the first decent day in a month and visited boat dealers in Alexandria and Fergus Falls.

We finally settled on an eighteen-foot Lund with a sixty-horsepower Mercury and a small electric trolling motor. We were both a bit embarrassed at the size of the motor, but the sixty horse power came with the package. The young salesman told us enthusiastically that it would be great for water sports. "Guess you'll have to learn how to water ski," I said to Rolf.

The boat had two fixed bench seats amidships, a control console at the right, and a moveable swivel seat that fit either forward or astern near the motor. There was a carpeted floor over the steel hull—no more tripping over the lateral hull frames—and a built-in live box behind the pilot. The price tag on our new joint toy was about $15,000 delivered to our place. Despite a high-pressure sales pitch we rejected a fish finding radar—unsporting—and a Global Positioning System. Even at out advanced age we were unlikely to get lost on Ten Mile Lake and be unable to plot a course back to the dock. The boat would arrive in about six weeks, shortly before the ice went out.

"It cost as much as my knee," Rolf noted with some wonder.

"But it'll be a lot more fun than your knee."

Tickled with ourselves, we stopped at the Municipal Liquor Store in Fergus for what we considered one of the basic food groups—spirits.

Municipal liquor outlets had been one of the anomalies of this part of the state. "It's the Lutherans," I declared, "hardest dry-voting boozers in all Christendom."

"Why blame us?" Rolf protested. "My kin never drank."

"Well if they were afflicted with sobriety they weren't related to the Lutherans up here."

I told him how I used to share a nip with an old farmer whose slough I rented many years ago. He'd be plowing his land adjacent to my blind and I'd wave him over on a fall day. It wasn't hard. "Have a shot, Ed" He'd have about six while we discussed world problems, and then stagger back to his tractor. When I looked at the bottle to see what was left there was tobacco juice running down inside the neck.

It wasn't until the 1980s that a few sit-down restaurants with bars were allowed here about. Even now the steak house at the resort only served beer, wine and set-ups. But many brought their own bottles of hard liquor, purchased at the municipal liquor outlet in Fergus, Dalton, or Elbow Lake.

Rolf explained the phenomenon with a puckish grin: "The Lutheran Scandinavians knew that you Irish would eventually invade the area, and they needed some control over your drinking habit." They were also smart enough to finance many government services by the sale of booze. Something the Irish never would have taken the time to appreciate.

So we went home a jolly crew, excited about our new acquisition and tired from the shopping adventure. That called for a late afternoon nap. Not to be confused with our morning drowsy time.

The last day of February was the state deadline for the removal of icehouses from the lake, and we watched the flurry of activity through our glass doors with sneering enthusiasm. Some had to be hacked loose from the grip of the lake. A few ice shacks came apart and wheels spun as vehicles labored. In Rolf's estimation the fools were finally getting their comeuppance. "Shouldn't have been there anyway. Making a mess out of our lake."

Even Tina got into the act, growling at the unaccustomed activity. "Good dog," Rolf encouraged her. When the last structure was gone Rolf said, "There," as if *he* had decreed the removal.

The final days of February had provided a few views of the sun and a bit of a thaw. March held the promise of more warmth but it was a snowy month and the roads and our driveway remained ice rinks. Rolf's knee was healing rapidly but he remained pretty much house bound, fearful of a fall that could set him back.

The next project calculated to kill time and speed the advent of spring was the organization of our fishing tackle. We checked line, artificial lures, leaders, weights, hooks, and oiled our reels. We also verified the presence of bottle openers, our lifetime old geezer licenses, and sharpened the filleting knives. The missing items were listed and a supply run was planned to Fergus to replenish stocks. Busy, busy.

We had spent so much time in the sporting good department of the Fleet Farm store that the help called us by our first names. Before leaving town we stopped at the super market. Rolf was feeling confident enough of his new knee that he was the cart pusher in each store.

In the meat department I noted the frozen walleye pike filets. (We had long since run out of our own supply.) "My God, they're from Canada," Rolf marveled. "And us right here in pike country." But he was opposed to buying any as extravagant. "We'll have them in the freezer soon enough. And at the cost of a little bait."

"And," I added, "a $15,000 boat."

Then I spotted some lutefisk in a freezer, and kidded Rolf. "How about some dried cod treated with lye? Doesn't that prospect make you smack your Norsk lips?"

"No," he said gravely, uninsulted, "My parents ate it once in a great while, but I couldn't even stand the smell. It was like something the cat had dragged in. Actually, Mike, I never ate much fish until you started cooking for me. I really enjoy your way of doing it."

"You're not going to hug me right here in front of all of Fergus Falls?"

"Perish the thought. Vikings don't hug."

"Did they high-five?"

"No," he responded as if the expert on all things Viking, "they just head butted."

"I'll take your word for it."

EIGHTEEN

THE FIRST LIGHT OF A NEW DAY invaded the house giving relief to various dark objects. I had not moved except for the silent act of opening my eyelids. There was Tina, wide-awake on her bed, observing me with those big brown eyes. Like most non-nocturnal animals she rose and rested with the sun, but how could she always be awake before me, waiting in joyous anticipation for her buddy to begin the day's adventure?

As I swung my legs to the floor we began a precise ritual. Tina rose, tail wagging furiously, and sat in front of me. "Good morning, Tina."

"Uh-uh-uh," she responded. Then she buried her head between my knees for a scratch of neck and ears. When I finished with a pat on her shoulders, she got up and allowed me to rise. I did so like the Tin Man, my joints resisting this first attempt at extension. I staggered a few feet then bent over slowly until my fingertips touched the floor. *Hold it*. Then stretched back up straight and arched my spine. It always had the same effect. There were little electric shock waves from the lumbar region to the hip and down the right leg. It was my ancient, gnarled vertebra pressing on wires in the central nervous system. One could experience similar electric jolts by swinging an ax and hitting a rock, or cracking the elbow on a solid object—the infamous crazy bone sensation.

While I went through my unlimbering ritual, Tina performed hers: stretching her front and back legs to near full extension as she emitted a sound that was half groan and half yawn. Then she shook her great head hard enough, I would think, to dislodge her brain. After swallowing my daily anti-inflammatory—doing my bit for the poor pharmaceutical industry—I pulled on my clothes, and we went to the kitchen door to confront the new day.

Tina bounded off a short distance through the dirty snow to her favorite pee spot and then maneuvered endlessly for just the right location for a crap. I observed the day from the rear stoop and edged into the semi-light that was so gray it seemed out of focus. Fog had settled on the land surrounding Ten Mile Lake, and being the first we had seen in some months, it took me a time to realize that this signaled a warming. Perhaps we might yet feel that Chinook wind.

The sun did its business of burning off the fog, and since it was attaining a higher angle, it began the invisible process of burning the ice. Now as March advanced, we looked out at a lake crust that was neither white nor silver but pewter.

Toward the end of the month a wet snow had morphed into a rain. And although it froze that night, turning the country into a giant skating rink, it was clear that arctic weather had lost its grip. Could spring and boating be far off?

We were like children attempting to will something to happen: *rain, rain, go away*. But us old goats were imploring the lake to open. "I think I can just see a hole toward the center of the lake. Well maybe not." "Is there water near the shore yet?" We could speculate endlessly on the probability that the lake's crust would break up on this or that day. "By next week it will be cracking for sure." We needed that Chinook wind. And indeed, a soaking rain fell on the 29th of March, vanquishing the snow, except for drifts in roadside ditches. Warm water on the top of the ice, in combination with a longer lasting sun, was a great icebreaker.

It got so balmy on April 1st, relatively speaking, that we ventured out on the deck after supper. It was about fifty degrees. Tina cuddled between us. This was her kind of weather. We toasted ourselves for having survived winter on the tundra and sat in our deck chairs gazing into the already darkening sky. Minnesotans greeted the advent of spring with such relish because of what we had been obliged to endure.

It was 8:30 p.m. when the phone rang, jangling our tranquility. Both of us winced, looked at the phone angrily and then at each other. *What the hell!* Phone calls were rare enough. But one this late was either a wrong number or trouble. It was the latter.

Ida Hansen wanted us to know that Paul had suffered a heart attack and was in a hospital at Fort Myers, Florida. The para-medics got to them in time, but he would be having bypass surgery. Both of their daughters, Carol and Bonnie, were flying down. Ida didn't know how long it would be until they returned. Could we continue to house Tina? Of course, I assured her. And we would continue to keep watch on the house and mow the grass when that was needed. "We'll be holding a good thought over you. Take care, Ida, and stay in touch."

I told Rolf the gist of the call, and he shook his head. "How can that be? He was such a healthy looking guy."

"Not like us creaking old farts," I agreed, as we ruminated on the bad fortune of our friend.

The next day the boat was delivered, and the dealer left it on the front lawn aboard a new trailer. He took the old boat and its trailer as a trade-in. When we had water, I would launch the dock and the boat. In the meantime, Rolf was determined to get in the boat and do some dry land sailing. With the aid of a stepladder we both boarded. Tina ran around the boat and barked until I got out and lifted her inside. She gave the new rig a thorough sniff test then assumed her navigational post at the bow. What a goofy trio we must have seemed to passing neighbors, sitting in our boat in the yard in forty-degree weather as if we were part of a naval review.

"We need a map of the lake," Rolf had insisted for the umpteenth time, despite my vast experience on these waters. We needed some supplies anyway, and off we went to Fergus for TV dinners and a map.

It was another warm day, and the wind began blowing from the northwest. "This ought to break up the ice," Rolf said. Sure enough, on our return there was a great patch of open water at the north end of the lake and waves were battling against the ice shelf. "See," Rolf said, like some sort of Nordic Nostradamus.

That night the wind swung around to the southwest hastening the ice breakup. Great chunks split off and began crunching and grinding against others. It sounded like a demolition derby.

Rolf pored over the lake map that night. I pointed out the depths and the locations that were historically the best fishing grounds. But his concentration kept returning to the big island across the way. He was back on that subject after a winter lay-off. He pointed. *Had I ever been on this or that shore?* It looked like there was a causeway onto the island on the west. *Had I ever been there?* I was dismissive of his probing questions but assured him that we would conduct a modest reconnaissance from the boat when we could get out on the water. As it turned out, there would be nothing modest about it.

About noon the next day we got another call from Ida. Paul's surgery went well and he was doing fine. She was well and the girls were there. But he couldn't travel, and their return was now indefinite. Again I urged her not to worry about anything here but to keep us apprised of Paul's condition.

"It's a fine thing to see a family rallying like that," I said to Rolf. "Loyalty," he declared. It was his anthem.

NINETEEN

UNSEASONABLY WARM WEATHER favored us in early April and, with the help of south winds, the lake ice was vanquished over the course of a few days. When we arose on the 10th of April to find open water as far as we could see, we hurried through breakfast and went out to play in the water like kids. First order of business was to give Tina some water retrieves with her plastic training dummy. Despite the stunning cold of the recently iced water, she bounded into the lake with unbridled joy and returned to shore with a mighty shake of her coat, preparatory to going right back in. She would have done this endlessly had my arm not tired. Next, we rolled the dock in and staked it down. Then we towed the trailer to the public landing just a quarter-mile south. I drove the truck back to the house and Rolf had the honor of skippering the boat back to the dock on its maiden voyage.

Our first fishing trip was delayed just long enough for us to make a run to the bait store. While I went for night crawlers and some store-bought sandwiches, Rolf gathered our gear in the boat. We added some beer to the live box and briefly considered what essential item might be missing. As with hunting, organizing for a fishing trip was part of the attraction, but breathless anticipation frequently overcomes sound planning. Finally, we cast off, Tina ensconced in the bow, and all three of us thrilled. The boat handled beautifully, and we were as comfortable as anyone could be in an open vessel.

We puttered about the lake diligently, trolling first, then anchoring where I believed there was a crappie hole. The walleye season didn't open for another couple of weeks. We could see a few folks fishing from shore off the road near the resort, but there was only one other boat on the lake. A persistent chop and a rising breeze began to chill our bones. And there were no strikes.

A huge flock of migratory ducks came into the lake and some local geese passed over, honking to each other, mocking the two old fools and the dog in the boat. The fish, however, remained elusive.

"I think the fish may not have come north yet," was my rationale. My hands were beginning to freeze and my early enthusiasm was evaporating. It would have been hard to hold a cold can of beer. "We should have brought a thermos of coffee," I suggested. There was no response from Rolf. Damned if he'd cry uncle. I should have realized that I couldn't get into a contest with him over getting cold and retreating. People who bore the genes of those who had sailed from Norway to North America were not likely to bitch about a little forty-degree weather.

Finally, after two hours of frigid fishing, I pleaded for a return. As great as the new boat was it afforded no protection from the elements. Rolf seemed to agree too quickly, but he had won the contest of wills.

The wind was on shore, the controls were still new to me, and I landed our new boat like it was the Ile de France, crashing the dock.

It wasn't until we were ashore that Rolf said, "Bumpers, that's what we also forgot." It was a thinly veiled insult regarding my seamanship, but he was right. I had taken them off the old boat and hung them in the garage. But there was no serious damage done to either the new boat or the dock. Like the first scuff on a new car, it was now behind me and my future ship handling would undoubtedly be flawless.

No sooner did I have myself thawed than Tina was pestering me for some more play in the lake. It took several outings, but she settled in early that evening, content to be back at her water work. "Ah, the smell of wet Labrador," I intoned. There was something about that musty odor that was strangely satisfying to me but could not be explained to a non-dog lover. It was an acquired appreciation.

The next morning we tried again. There was less wind, more sun, and we were dressed more warmly and had forsaken the beer for a thermos of coffee. I caught a small walleye and released it. And Rolf landed and released a nice small-mouth bass also out of season. He had thrown every lure in his tackle box into the lake and finally wearied of the effort and asked to go ashore for a pee. "Just nose into the island," he suggested, no point in going back to the cabin.

I had my suspicions, but nonetheless put the bow of the boat on the north shore of the island while Rolf clambered out with a mooring line. As soon as I was ashore, Rolf said he would, "Just look around."

"What is there to see? It's uninhabited."

"You can wait while I scout." And off he went, lost from view in a matter of seconds. I hung onto Tina for fear she would try to follow or lead and get lost. It would have been easy. The island was anchored by a dense growth of budding, mostly deciduous, trees: oak, cottonwood, poplar, ash, and maple interspersed with spindly spruce trees. The trees had grown close together. Even some dead trees had been held temporarily upright by healthy neighbors. Other dead falls had hit the forest floor at crazy angles making any trek by foot a challenge. There were still patches of snow on the ground and little apparent ground cover. The summer overhead canopy had not permitted grass or weeds to flourish.

Tina whined to be part of whatever Rolf was doing. Surely it was a hunt. And I whined too. *"Why the hell did I let him go? The old fart has a new knee. This wasn't exactly a stroll in the park. Will he be able to find his way back?"* After about ten minutes Tina raised her head and cocked her ears. She had a bead on him coming through the trees a full half minute before I could see him and greeted him with a great spate of panting, happy to see him and sure that he had been on some adventure without his trusty Labrador.

"Well," I said sarcastically, "did you discover the lost city of the Vikings?"

Rolf ignored my remark as he untied the boat and climbed over the bow. "Those trees are almost as thick as the reeds in the slough near Four Mile Lake. I started too far to the east to get much of anywhere. Next time we'll begin further west."

"To what purpose?"

"We just need to know what's there?"

I had learned long ago not to argue with him when he had his mind set on something. All I could do was hope that he would lose interest or become distracted. Fat chance.

That evening we sat on the deck in the fading light and mapped our next assault on the fish. I had plans to find that crappie hole, but Rolf seemed preoccupied. He nodded agreement with whatever I proposed but really was focusing on the island across the way. He watched it as if he expected a Panzer tank to appear on the shore, traversing its turret and elevating its cannon.

Whatever diverse plans we may have had they would have to wait. That morning we awoke to thunder. A storm rolled through and then heavy rain descended like a gray curtain. It rained without letup, the famous April showers, for three days. As fishing crazy as we were, it was like our chosen profession, we declined to sit in a downpour to possibly catch some fish we considered second rate.

The steady rain already had us bunkered in the cabin, depressed and getting fidgety, when the phone rang like an alarm. "Mike, this is Carol Burroughs . . ." She hesitated. "Ida's daughter."

"Oh, yes Carol," I finally got my head in gear. "I thought you were an aluminum siding salesman. How's everything?"

There were a few seconds of ominous silence, and I thought I heard a sob, "Mom asked that I call you. Dad had a massive coronary and died yesterday."

"Oh, God, no." I gulped for air. "It can't be."

"He went quickly. He was in the hospital but there was nothing the doctors could do."

I stumbled through my emotions to express regrets, saying those words we babble at such a time. She told me that they were returning to Minnesota that night and gave me details regarding the funeral in St. Paul.

A few days later the three of us set out for the Cities. Tina came along since we couldn't leave her behind. We planned to attend the wake and return that night. Rolf and I were depressed at the loss of our friend and what lay ahead. We said little. But Tina, in her blessed ignorance, was her usual upbeat self.

It was a dreary day in St.Paul where the rain had preceded us. The wake, scheduled from 4:00 to 8:00 p.m., was at Wilwerscheid's on Grand Avenue, and the parking lot was nearly full when we arrived about 4:30. We walked Tina a bit, postponing the inevitable chore, then put her back in the truck. The place was thronged by a legion of sad faces. Paul and Ida had been lifelong residents of St. Paul until their retirement to the lake, and their daughters had been raised here.

There amidst the sadness was Ida with that great warm smile, greeting people and putting them at ease as they mouthed the customary condolences. There were a lot of suits in the room and us country bumpkins looked a little out of place, but when it was our turn, Ida greeted us like we were royalty. Rolf stammered his regrets as he stood stiffly. He had only known Paul for a short time. But she reached out and hugged him, commenting on how well he was walking since our last gala meeting. I was your typical Irishman—once I stood before her my emotions erupted. I could not express a thought through my grief, just tried to hold back my tears and be as brave as she was. She gave me a hug, protesting that we should not have come all the way down to St. Paul. I swore that we would be there for her when she got back and would do anything and everything possible to help. As others pressed behind us to pay their respects she said: "Don't be so sad, Mike. We had a wonderful life and were blessed with this magnificent family and great friends like you." How typical of Ida to succor the mourner.

Carol and Bonnie, with their husbands and a raft of grand-children were hovering nearby. The girls also gave us a lot more than we gave them, and we promised to take care of things at the lake. There was no mention of Tina, a subject I had been nervously anticipating, and no discussion of Ida's lake plans. After saluting the flag draped coffin we got out of the way.

As usual, Tina was unfailingly happy when we returned to her in the truck, and I thought it was good that we were unable to explain the loss of her dear master. For her well of devotion was probably greater than we could comprehend. We drove in silence for some time and finally Rolf said, "What a fine life they had, having each other and those kids. I'm so envious."

"And why him," I asked, "and not one of us to the happy hunting ground? He left so much behind. There's no one to mourn me."

"Me and Tina would miss you, you old goat." It was the most affectionate thing Rolf had ever said to me.

TWENTY

LTHOUGH WE WERE STILL brooding over the passing of Paul Hansen, all the inevitable signs of new life were flourishing at the lake. The recent rains had caused the grass to end its dormancy, and the trees were shooting out new growth. There were several cottonwoods on my north and south property lines and two near the lakeshore at either corner that displayed long shiny buds.

I had erected a wood duck house in a cottonwood nearly overhanging the lake, and now a pair of migratory wood ducks took up residence, delighting us with their comings and goings. This breed would fly right through the four-inch entrance hole making a cartoon-like landing. As soon as they arrived, the "woodies" began to clean house, tossing out last year's bedding as they squealed at each other. (Wood ducks have more of a chirp than a quack.) In about three weeks their ducklings would be ready to venture into the world. The adults would kick them out unceremoniously and the chicks would fall like small rocks, their fuzzy wings flapping furiously. (I wondered if they cried out the duck equivalent of "Geronimo" as they descended.) The drake and hen would then gather them up like a kid's pull toy and escort them out single file onto the lake for a campout in the reeds. There they would grow, exchange their fuzz for feathers, and learn about ducking.

A few lilacs I had planted three years ago gave promise of blooming, and the woodchucks that wintered deep in the ground under my woodpile emerged to give Tina a new duty. She first spotted them from the deck and with a great skidding of her paws she scampered down the steps and charged the stack. The rodents would dive in their holes long before Tina arrived, but she never gave up hope of a possible retrieve. Rolf would give a disdainful "Ahc" at the performance, but Tina was never discouraged. She considered critter defense part of her responsibility, just like wading in the shallow off-shore water searching for intruding minnows. Every now and then she would bury her head in the lake then pull back with what sounded like "SNORF," spraying out water, snoot juice, and possibly a tadpole.

I often wondered what she might do with a large fish if one swam close enough. Retrieving fish in the Canadian Maritime Provinces had been part of the early history of the working breed. Tina was mightily interested in any fish that we caught, anxious to take them on and stop that damn floppiness with a good headshake. We didn't let her. But after clearing away any hooks we did allow her a sniff and a sneaky lick. She smelled enough like fish without chewing on them.

A pair of loons arrived to establish their dominance over the lower end of the Ten Mile, and we delighted in their haunting call, so uniquely part of the Minnesota lake experience. Indeed, the loon had been declared the state bird one year by a legislature that had absolutely nothing better to do.

We also saw activity by local geese, the ones from the Otter Tail Power reservoir that wintered there in the plant's warm water. They were mostly in pairs now, searching for fresh feed and scouting a place to nest. Honkers intent on mating flitted about, examining housing prospects in weedy bays and incongruous places like farm fields. We even spotted a big Canada on a garage roof, looking over a lakeshore lot. High overhead their migratory brethren, traveling up the Mississippi flyway, appeared in great echelons as they returned from the Gulf Coast and Mexico. Sometimes these snow and Canada geese were so high that we would not have seen them had it not been for their collective dog-like chatter. Guided by an unerring internal navigation system, they labored toward the edge of the frozen lakes far to the north.

A necessary spring chore for us lake dwellers was the lowering of our high-rise birdhouse for cleaning, an essential to getting a new batch of purple martins. Virtually every home on the lake had erected a hinged birdhouse that provided a cluster of apartments for the martins. These small, nimble birds could eat there weight in mosquitoes each day, and along with grass mowing, they were essential to enjoyment of the summer at lakeside. When at their acrobatic work, purple martins skimmed about the land and water, scooping up the irritating mosquitoes. No one used foggers, which could make people sick, and no one used bug zappers which only attracted bugs that otherwise required a blind search for human blood.

We also cleaned Hansen's birdhouse in preparation for Ida's return, cleared some straw covering off her flower bed, and we checked the place as we had promised, making sure that doors were secure and the paper box empty.

Awaiting Ida's return, in early May we continued to busy ourselves with angling. Cool weather had not yet released its hold on the area, and fishing was only for Vikings and a few resolute companions. The pike opener was still a week away and the bass were not being cooperative. So we concentrated on finding that crappie hole that had so far eluded us. I had located it several years ago and returned to the spot I had mentally marked on the lake using shore references: a clump of pine here, an old silo there. But either my memory had faded or the hole had moved. With Rolf using a weighted line and me maneuvering the boat slowly, we probed for it like a

Polish mine sweeper crew. When at last the weighted line seemed to fall over a cliff we dropped anchor and deployed some worms.

Almost immediately we each got action, feeling vindicated that we had not spent $250 dollars on a depth finder. We had justified saving that money for life's essentials like beer, scotch, and cigars. Within an hour of cold work we had caught four keepers and released another half dozen. We joked about painting an X on the floor of the boat to mark the spot but satisfied ourselves with a more precise triangulation from some west shore buildings, a cluster of tall pine on the east shore and that south silo.

As we weighed anchor, Rolf said, "Let's swing over to the island for another look." Chilly as I was, I knew that we would go back to the island sooner or later. It might as well be now. This time we nosed in closer to the northwest estuary that barely connected the island to the lakeshore. There were heavy reed banks guarding all but this north shoreline, thus it seemed the only easy place to land a boat.

Rolf climbed off with a mooring line right behind Tina who eagerly vaulted ashore. As Rolf was securing the boat to a tree, he called, "Come on," to me over his shoulder.

I said, "Now wait a minute." And rummaged in my tackle box for a dog whistle for what I knew was an inevitable trek. "She's crazier for this sort of expedition than you are. She thinks we're actually looking for something."

When we were all assembled Rolf said, "This way," just as if he had a specific destination, and we took a west heading. While the foliage was not yet full, the overhead was still obscured by the budding leaves, leaving the ground fairly dark. The tangle of densely packed trees, saplings, and fallen timber was just as it appeared from the lake. Tina dashed ahead, over and under the obstructions, and Rolf did almost as well with a sort of crouching serpentine movement. I could imagine him in combat fatigues and helmet going through Europe like that.

"Slow down, damn it!" Then to myself, *"There's not enough room in here to swing a cat."* I was fumbling like an old man, tripping as I climbed over dead falls. I gave a few toots of the whistle and Tina reappeared momentarily to check on us then continued her frolic through the forest.

Rolf hesitated, out of respect for his elder partner I assume, and said, "We're coming to a clearing."

"How can you tell that?" You couldn't see ten feet forward.

"I can see some sky ahead," and he pointed upward at about a forty-five-degree angle.

Sure enough, after a few more paces we entered a little weed-covered clearing, devoid of trees or anything else. There was still a little dirty snow present but no sign of any human activity, only a faint path as wide as a set of tire tracks that led to the small causeway. That skinny strip of ground, barely eight feet wide and about fifteen feet long, was just above lake level. "You had better be sober if you try to drive in here," I said by way of debunking any theory about automobile lights. Rolf grunted in what I presumed was agreement. Tina looked up at me expectantly, tail wagging: *"Now what?"* she seemed to be asking.

"Did you expect to find the Lost Dutchman, or possibly Jimmy Hoffa?" I asked sarcastically.

No response and apparently no offense taken.

After a few minutes of silent inspection by our party of Boy Scouts, Rolf finally said, "Okay," and started back in the general direction of the boat. We debarked and headed for the dock only some half-mile away.

He was silent for some time, no different than usual, but kept his eye on the island as we departed and after we were back at the house. I believe he was trying to visually survey where we had been in relation to where he had seen the lights.

I felt certain we would have returned to Rolf's island of mystery the next day. He mused on the matter interminably. But our attention was diverted by a bustle of activity on the lake at the scene of our past glory. A flotilla of sizable boats and pontoons appeared to recover the Haugen snow mobile that had gone through the ice back in December. It was a daylong operation in which divers located the rig, attached some flotation devices and brought the snow mobile to the surface. After towing the whole mess to the public landing, the errant machine was beached and hauled away, probably ruined by its long immersion. However, it would no longer leak gasoline or snag trolled fishing gear. We, of course, took a proprietary interest in the entire operation, supervising from the cabin deck.

Then for several days more spring rains came, hard and steady, dropping a gray veil over the lake. In the middle of our seventies we had now grown enough brains, or at least retained sufficient gray matter, that prevented us from fishing in a cold, soaking downpour. We could only watch the grass and nearby trees burst forth with a lustrous display of green.

TWENTY-ONE

It was late afternoon, the day before the pike opener, when a car pulled into our driveway. Ida had returned, along with part of her clan, and just wanted us to know she was there and relieve us from house-watching duty.

"How are you doing?" we chorused, after the preliminaries. She was still beautiful, vibrant Ida, a smile on her face. But, I thought, she was looking a bit sad about the eyes.

"Oh, you know, it's been awhile now. I lived with concern ever since Paul's first heart attack. Knew how vulnerable we were at our age. And I have the kids, who have just been wonderful. Bonnie's with me now for a few days. They'll have to let go of me here sooner or later and get back to their lives. But I'll be okay. Don't worry." Like we needed comfort.

We talked over each other insisting that we were here and prepared to look after her, and how she wasn't to mow any grass or chop any wood. "I know. You're both dear friends. Thanks." She put out a hand to each of us and gave a soft squeeze.

Did she need us or did us emotional cripples need her? It seemed that we required someone to save after years of failing the obligations in our relationships. What a pair of sorry old wrecks we were.

Through all of this discussion Tina had been pirouetting among us, happy as a clam and thrilled to be inhaling Ida's familiar scent. "Shall I get Tina's gear?" I finally asked, trying to seem natural but secretly dreading the answer.

127

"Oh, Mike," Ida stroked the black head, "I've thought about it a lot. Selfishly, I'd like the companionship after the family leaves. But she would be better off with you. I'm starting to have a little hip trouble. I can't give her the care that you can, the Labrador quality of life. Would you keep her and I'll just come for a visit now and then? Would that be asking too much?"

I was stammering and shaking my head, not wishing to seem too delighted, but had to do a double take at Rolf, who was talking over me. "She's no trouble. That would be just fine. We'll take good care of her."

"Wonderful. Bless you both. And you too, Tina." She knelt for a dog smooch as I repeated to Bonnie that we should be considered Ida's personal staff of servants and guardians.

Back inside Rolf said, "We can manage with the dog. It'll be all right."

"Well of course we can, but I didn't think you liked Tina that much." Tina looked from one of us to the other at the mention of her name.

"What ever gave you that idea," Rolf said. I didn't have an equivalent for "Ahc" or I might have used it just then.

THE FISHING OPENER BROUGHT AN ARMADA to Ten Mile Lake. Boats and anglers were so numerous that it was possible their gross displacement had raised the lake level a few inches. It took precise boat handling to keep the hundreds of trolled fishing lines from getting tangled. And then there were the few ninnies who had to go everywhere at full throttle, oblivious of their wake and its effect on other boats. It was classic weather for the annual event: cool and partly cloudy with a northwest breeze that fostered the infamous walleye chop.

After fishing since sunrise we only had two modest keepers, had released several small fry and exhausted the coffee thermos and goodie supply. Returning to the dock, we relieved ourselves, got warm, packed lunch and beer and sallied forth once more. Tina was eagerly anticipating lunch snacks. Food was always near the top of her agenda.

The sky had cleared, and as we trolled south out of the breeze. The warmth was so pleasant that we were reluctant to get back into the prime fishing grounds in the wind with all the boat traffic. We broke out the lunch sooner than anticipated and each cracked open a beer. Trolling lines snared the inevitable snags in the shallow waters of the south bay, but we were cozy and out of the chop and the boat wakes and entered into that province of fishing where you didn't much give a damn if you got a bite.

"Nice to be out of the wind," Rolf commented from his stern chair. "Let's cruise around the bottom of the island and up toward that causeway."

"Here we go again." His reconnaissance of that damn island was still not complete.

I brought the boat slowly up the west side of the island, reeling in my line in the narrow passage, as Rolf shifted himself and his line to his perch in the bow. We approached the barely discernible causeway, the weedy lake bottom becoming more visible. I began to cautiously turn the boat, telling Rolf, "I'm afraid we'll get the prop tangled in weeds if we go further." He reeled in his line and then, as our bow came about, he cast a floater back toward the causeway.

"Now we've been around this island on all sides and still no sign of any people."

"Except for those two," Rolf responded.

"What two? Where?"

"Just onto the island, in the shade of that giant oak, just under that big horizontal left branch."

"I don't see anything."

"There's a pair of big guys standing there looking toward us, all in black, hard to see them in the shade. About 200 feet away."

"Rolf, I still don't see anything. How did you spot them?"

"There was a momentary reflection off some sun glasses. Now they're backing deeper into the woods."

I strained again and just caught a glimpse of movement before the forest shadows enveloped them. The trained eye of the old infantryman had indeed seen something.

We moseyed back around the island, past the dam and back up the channel, trying various baits and lures without success. Brushing the reed beds, we had to clean weeds off the hooks, and lost some bait in the process. As we returned toward the mouth of the bay and the swarm of fishing boats, Rolf got a strike and had a memorable fight with a northern. It was fifteen minutes of battle before we got him alongside the boat and could see the size of the lunker. A mean twenty-five-pounder with rows of razor-like teeth, it flopped about in the bottom of the boat and threatened to evict us. Tina almost got caught in the landing net as she attempted to help. The three of us finally managed to get the fish into the live box.

"That calls for a beer," Rolf said triumphantly and reached into the live box that also served as our cooler. There was a thrashing of water as he yanked out the plastic six-pack holder "The Sombitch tried to bite me!"

"That was a close call. He almost got your beer."

Chuckling, we toasted each other as the vicious pike banged against the wall. Damn but he was mad. With each thump Tina wanted to go into the box and kick ass. The battle had drained our adrenaline reserve and, since it was past our naptime, we trolled our way toward the dock.

That evening, after a dinner of fresh pike fillets, we relaxed on the deck and reviewed the fleet of fishing boats still dragging the lake bottom. The days were getting longer now and we cherished the sunset routine even if it was a tad cool.

"You know," Rolf said with a tone of inevitability, "we have to go back there and see what those guys were doing." For a change, he was staring at the island.

"No, I don't know that we have to. Who put us in charge of that island? Why should we care?"

"Because," he said as if addressing an idiot child, "we are the only ones who know that something is going on over there. And it's probably criminal."

"Slow down a minute. We don't know that something criminal is going on over there. It could just be a couple of reprobates like us who go there to drink. They don't have a nice lake cabin like we do. So they get away from their wives on the island. And even if they were brewing moonshine, what business is it of ours? Why this obsession?"

"Curiosity. How do you think the Norsemen discovered America?"

"I always assumed they took a wrong turn leaving Greenland."

Rolf was neither amused nor offended. "We'll just have another little look. And you can stay in the boat if you want."

So the next day we set out to explore, disguised as fishermen. Rolf tied the bow and Tina was frantic to get out and join in his expedition, so I relented and followed. We had landed at the northwest corner of the island nearest to the clearing we had seen on the earlier trek. Given several more days of growing weather the forest had leafed out substantially and provided an overhead canopy that shaded the ground. It only took us a few seconds thrashing through the trees to reach the clearing.

Rolf stopped dead as we reached our goal. "What is that?" We approached a large black, box-like structure with a white top.

"Looks like a druid altar," I suggested, trying to maintain a degree of levity. On closer inspection the object turned out to be a five-by-six-by-eight-foot aluminum trailer of the type one might rent from U-Haul. It had two pair of tandem wheels and a hitch pointed toward the narrow road. The tongue of the hitch was propped on a log. A substantial padlock secured the rear doors. There were no license plates or any printing on the box except for a small manufacturer's plate.

Rolf put his chin in his hand for some heavy ruminating while he circled the trailer. I walked around the clearing to make sure that nothing else—animal, mineral, or vegetable—had manifested itself since our last visit. There seemed to be nothing but the black trailer. It wasn't a camper, although almost big enough to be one. Thumping the four walls and kicking the tires was a useless exercise that satisfied some curious inner urge but confirmed nothing. Rolf even sniffed at the back doors in an attempt to discern the contents. "Be careful what you wish for," I cautioned, but he shook his head and shrugged his shoulders. Nada. I examined the narrow track that led to the causeway, and it was apparent from the crushed grass that a vehicle had recently been driven across and turned around in the clearing. "Well the trailer wasn't parachuted in here," I submitted.

After a lot of mutual harumphing and ahcing we returned to the boat and boarded in silence. Rolf quickly cast out his favorite floater, maintaining our cover as fishermen, before I could even get the boat underway.

TWENTY-TWO

KNOWING THAT BONNIE HAD gone back to the Cities, we invited Ida out for a Saturday dinner at the resort. She had told us that the whole family was due up for a long weekend around the Fourth of July, so although we checked in with her most every day, we thought it would be good for her to get out a bit. We didn't want to invite ourselves over for a meal, and God forbid I should cook for a woman who was a gourmet chef.

Ida had a glass of wine while Rolf and I nursed our usual beers as we waited for our food. It had been hard to chat because people she knew kept dropping by to welcome her back and/or extend their condolences. When the three of us were finally by ourselves she said, "I've got something to tell you." It had an unpleasant ring to it. "I've decided to sell the house and move back to the Cities."

Rolf and I were both saddened but not surprised. Despite our attempts to help her with the chores and errands, she was alone in the boondocks. She went on to explain that her kids wanted her closer to them, and she was likely going to need a hip operation in the future. So considering her age, similar to ours, she felt it was practical to get an apartment or townhouse back in St. Paul. We, of course, said that we understood. But her absence would leave yet another void in our miserable lives.

As we left the steak house, Deputy Sheriff Ed Lindquist and his fancy wife were just arriving. We cornered him at the front door for just a second and, without divulging our repeated forays on to the island, told him of the lights we had seen there from our cabin. "Oh it's just probably kids having a beer party. I'll check it out. You guys shouldn't worry about it." Then he said, as if speaking to a pair of children, "Now, you boys won't go trespass over there?"

"Who us? Gosh no. We're just public spirited citizens conducting sort of a backwoods 'Neighborhood Watch.'"

On the way home Ida said, "What was all that about?" And we had to admit that we were doing some snooping on the island and had seen some peculiar things. I thought she might be critical, but she had also seen infrequent lights in the night from across the lake and wondered about the activity. We were reluctant to speculate and frighten her. Still I felt obliged to see her into the house, and Rolf walked around the place.

"Now be sure to lock up," I cautioned.

"Mike, I'm just fine. Don't you fuss about me."

Back at the cabin we commiserated about Ida's announcement then ruminated about the island. Rolf said, "Now what?" I had begun to share his fascination with the place and suggested that tomorrow we approach it from the south, its land link.

We spread a U.S. Geological Survey map on the table, pondered the matter and planned our next move. "We could also go to the county court house and check the ownership of the island." I could hardly believe I had said that. Rolf looked at me and a roguish grin rearranged his craggy features, like the cat that had swallowed the canary. He had finally roped me in. We were just like kids, becoming more intrigued now that we had been warned away. And we were graduating from being just inquisitive old farts to being naughty ones.

That Monday we went to the Registrar of Deeds office at the County Court House in Fergus and found that the uninhabited island was owned by the same family that farmed the adjacent land just south of the lake. It had all been in that clan for over a century, title passing to the current owner of record some ninety years ago. He had to be older than we were. Returning to the cabin, we took a route that would get us to the south end of Ten Mile Lake, turning on the county line road between Otter Tail and Grant Counties to look across the rolling fields that bordered on Ten Mile.

A north-south gravel road led across the field towards the lake and some farm buildings began to appear on the left. Beside an old sagging barn was a gray silo with a white metal cone partially open to the sky, no doubt in disuse like many others as farming had evolved from dairy herds to cash crops. From the lake I had seen the cap of that silo and glimpsed a nearby white farmhouse. They were some of the landmarks that had helped me triangulate my crappie hole.

We drove in despite signs urging us to keep out: "PRIVATE ROAD," "DEAD END." Hesitating, we looked at each other somewhat wide-eyed then mushed on cautiously, trying to appear as lost innocents. As the topography of the wheatfield slanted down toward the lake, we could see that the road forked, the well-worn left leg going into the farm structures, and the right track, little used and very weedy, dipping rapidly and bending toward the island. Almost immediately on taking the right fork we were out of sight of the farm buildings and descending toward the island. Within sight of the causeway, we came across an old gate made of wire and fence posts that had been intended as a barrier. But the gate had long since been rolled back, was tangled in weeds and vines, no longer an obstacle. Still the causeway was as we had seen it from prior reconnaissance: low, narrow, and almost awash.

I stopped and Rolf jumped out. "I'm going to have a look in the clearing," he said as he tiptoed through the boggy ground.

"Make it quick, we are decidedly trespassing."

He gave me a sort of dismissive wave as he proceeded onto the island. Tina whined to go with him as I turned the truck around, prepared for a rapid exit. Rolf returned shortly and jumped in. "The black trailer is still there," he proclaimed as we retraced our route back to the county line road, unchallenged.

THE DAYS WERE GETTING LONGER and the sunsets were glorious after a long tough winter. After dinner we sat in our deck chairs and enjoyed our spirits and cigars. A light breeze off the lake was waning but it still filled the air with the fruit of the cotton-woods, tiny puffs of fluff each transporting a pinhead-sized seed. If the botanical parachutists got close enough to Tina she would snap them out of the air. Ah the joys of spring.

"Now we have two mysteries," Rolf said, out of the blue. I knew he would be talking about the island and not really needing any response. So I took a sip of my Oban, a pull on my cigar, and blew a cloud of smoke out among the passing cottonwood seeds. Rolf continued: "Why is that trailer out there and how did they get it there? I think your pickup might get bogged down driving over that causeway, and every other approach is over water."

Three nights later we were again indulged in our relentless pursuit of indolence when I commented that we should be doing something more constructive. "An idle mind is the devil's workshop," I intoned, quoting my mother.

"My mind isn't idle," Rolf said a bit defensively.

"Well it's active as hell if you count obsessing over that island."

"What do you want me to do? Aren't we on summer vacation?"

He had me there. Still I felt the need of some additional mental stimulation and planned a trip to the library the following day. Rolf didn't want to go. I had not seen him read a book since he arrived here, but I badgered him into riding along.

As I assembled a few recent volumes by Jack Higgins, John LeCarre, and Alan Furst, Rolf moseyed aimlessly through the fine Fergus Falls library. At the checkout desk he appeared with a single soft-cover book. "That looks like good reading," the cute young librarian said, with a touch of sarcasm. He tucked it under his arm as we left but knew I was trying to read the cover, and he couldn't hide it forever. Giving me a sheepish look, like a fifteen-year-old caught with a girlie magazine, he held it up for my inspection: *Backyard Ballistics: How to Build a Potato Cannon*.

Rolf now had another interest: the assembly, operation and maintenance of a spud gun. Where he was going with this I didn't know, but since the new interest had blossomed on the basis of my urging, I could hardly refuse his request the next day to drive into the Fleet Farm store to buy the fixings for his project. On our return he busied himself at the workbench in the garage, cutting, gluing, and drilling various hunks of white plastic PVC pipe. I left him alone for some time, while I attended to my gardening chores, and then checked in to see what in God's name he was assembling. It resembled a World War II bazooka but was longer and all white. At its base was some bewildering mechanism the purpose of which was yet to be revealed.

Rolf looked up at me from his detailed labors. "Don't criticize now. You implied that I was idling, and now I'm busy."

"No, Tina thought you were idling. I thought you were fixating on that damn island. But now I see that I was wrong.

You're going to bombard it with potatoes, a healthy pastime for a growing boy. Reminds me of our old Fourth of July schemes when we were free to blow our fingers off without government interference."

After supper Rolf returned to the garage and his contraption. It was dark by the time he proclaimed his howitzer ready for action, so he agreed to wait until daylight for the first trial.

Although he was never one to loaf in the sack, Rolf was up before Tina and me. While I started coffee and some breakfast, he continued to tinker in the garage. Shortly he came inside and asked, "Got any potatoes?"

"About six."

"How about hair spray?"

"Now there you got me. What do you need with hair spray?"

"Propellant," he answered cheerily.

Later we stood in Ida's kitchen, twirling our caps. "Hair spray?" Her eyes shifted from one of us to the other, noting my curly gray hair and Rolf's silver crew cut.

Rolf examined the pattern in Ida's linoleum for so long that I was obliged to say, "It's for a project we're working on."

As she went down the hall to search I said, "Why don't you tell her?"

"Oh, you can."

"Well it's your cannon."

Ida heard my comment as she rounded the corner, a look on her face that I recall seeing from my mother whenever I was on the cusp of mischief. "Will half a can do?"

"Ahc, just fine," Rolf said. "We'll return it."

She pursed her lips to stifle a smile. "Need any styling mouse or eye liner?"

Rolf looked like he'd been caught with his hand in the cookie jar.

"What are you kids up to?" She could no longer contain that dazzling smile.

"Well," I intervened as, Rolf busily examined the can, "*we* are building a potato cannon. And hair spray is needed as the explosive charge." She covered her mouth to contain her mirth as I continued, "It's almost the Fourth, you know, and heaven forbid we should buy illegal fireworks."

"Good, I was afraid you might be doing something foolish. I'll keep my first aid kit handy."

She had the right idea. The spud gun looked like a dangerous contraption, a long tube supported by some scrap lumber and a lot of duct tape. Red Green would have been proud of Rolf's handiwork, although when set up it looked like a strong wind might dismantle it.

"Now until I can rig a proper base plate and tripod I need to be here (on his knees) in order to charge the gun, hold the tube, and fire. You need to watch the lake so some boat doesn't wander onto the range. Then you need to drop the shell (he meant the potato) down the tube when I say, then back away. He should have added that I was in charge of Tina's safety. She had been splashing in the lake, chasing rodents and generally ignoring the project until Rolf bent low to squirt a shot of hair spray into the nipple that led to the combustion chamber. Tina ran up bent her head low next to Rolf's and gave her head a mighty shake, slapping Rolf with her ears, as she inhaled a snoot full of Pantene. "Ahc, scoot."

We started all over. "Have you ever done anything like this before?" I thought it past due for me to question the coming experiment, but didn't want to be an, "I told you so," sort of guy.

Rolf looked at me like I was teched. "I had the combat infantry badge: proficient on all infantry weapons including the sixty-millimeter mortar. Now hang onto the dog and check the range."

"All clear!" I yelled, as Rolf shot another dose of spray into the bottom of the tube and Tina strained at her collar to help.

"Let her go" (the potato not Tina).

I dropped a large oblong baking spud down the tube and stepped back.

Rolf, still bent low over the base, held the tube with his left hand, and grasped the lantern sparker device in his right. "Fire in the hole!" he bellowed. Tina and I both jumped, startled by his roar.

Immediately there followed a *"PFUT"* sort of sound, and a slight wave of air hit me. We looked up along the expected path of the missile, mouths open, eyes shaded. Tina broke my grip and bolted for the lake, certain that she was needed to retrieve a shot duck.

After about five seconds of craning our necks back we chanced a momentary sideways glance at each other, then returned our gaze to the blue sky and its scattered white puffs of cumulus. "Do you see it?" Rolf asked hopefully.

"No."

"Neither do I," he admitted in a disappointed tone.

I turned my focus to the lake before us, looking for a splash or a widening ring on the relatively calm water. There was nothing but Tina dashing to and fro in the shallows looking for an elusive prey.

We finally stopped gawking into the empty lake and looked at each other in puzzlement. "She bucked pretty good," Rolf said, "but I had her aimed about twenty degrees off vertical. Where the hell did it go?"

"Either you shot a baking potato over toward Highway 59, or ..."

Rolf lowered the tube and looked down the muzzle. "Oh, the sombitch is still down there. Defective round. A hang fire."

We tipped the gun upside down and after some thunking a slightly bruised potato tumbled out. Tina pounced on it triumphantly. "Rolf, you've invented the world's largest, most cumbersome potato peeler."

"Ahc."

After retrieving the potato from Tina, Rolf concluded that the subject missile, scuffed and then chewed to death, was too big. The tube was two and one-half inches in diameter and the spud was a close match, except that it had gotten tilted and jammed. The gas had escaped around it but had not dislodged it. We likely needed better projectiles than the large, oblong baking potatoes at hand. We trimmed a skinnier spud for the second test shot. Again I took my post near the tube and held Tina. Rolf injected a load of hair spray, bellowed, "Fire in the hole!" and pulled the trigger. This time there was a hollow *FONG* sound and we scanned the sky.

"There," Rolf said pointing. I saw nothing but followed his line of vision. Ultimately we were rewarded with a waterspout and the concentric rings that followed some distance out on the lake. It had worked but wasn't as satisfying as our childhood Fourth of July adventures had been, blowing up tin cans, paper cartons, and crab apples.

"We need to think on this some more. Maybe I used too much propellant. The can's almost empty. And I need to perfect the base and the tripod. I'm all hunkered down when she goes off." And so it was back to town for some more equipment and supplies.

"Good thing we don't have jobs," I noted as we headed down I-94.

After picking up some additional sheet metal, stove bolts, lumber, and duct tape, we went to the grocery store. We'd been there the day before, so all we needed was our mortar supplies. We looked over the hair spray, all fourteen brands and variations.

"This is the one," Rolf intoned as he brandished a can of Aqua Net.

"Does the fine print say, 'Recommended for Potato Cannons'?"

"Better mix of things that ignite: propane, glycol, butane." He smiled. "Let's get a six pack. And we need to replace Ida's can."

The assortment of potato products was only slightly less confusing. There were red, yellow, baking, and Idaho or Red River russets. Again Rolf examined them with care and deliberation. "I think the Red Rivers or the yellows may be best. Sort of uniformly round. Let's get a bag of each."

"But we had trouble seeing the baking potatoes with the brown skin. These are going to be even tougher viewing against the sky."

"You're right, Rolf agreed. " How can we darken them? Paint?"

"How about we try some food coloring." *Did I say that?* I was aiding and abetting this silly project despite myself.

Of course we had to ask directions to the baking section and there found these tiny bottles of liquid coloring, the size of eyedroppers.

"Better get several," Rolf reasoned. "These spuds may soak that up like sponges."

The checkout girl viewed our selections on the belt: enough hairspray for a chorus line, sufficient potatoes for a church supper, and more food coloring than they had sold in the past year. She glanced at us as if we might be escapees from a lunatic asylum. We just smiled back. She began to scan our unusual purchases but kept glancing at us like we might conk her with a bag of North Dakota reds, blind her with hair spray, and shoot food coloring down her cleavage.

By late that afternoon Rolf had completed his modifications to the potato cannon, and a thing of beauty it was. He had used an old wheel rim from the garage as a base plate, lashing it with several thousand yards of duct tape; and improved the tripod with a sleeve and some set screws that permitted the elevation to be altered. After my mowing chores of the adjacent yards and Hansen's place were done, I was assigned the potato dye job, for which there was no manual.

Several test shots later we had perfected the gadget and confirmed that the Red River Russets were the most reliable projectiles and, with my expert dye job (they resembled lumps of coal), we could actually follow the "fall of shot," as they say in the navy.

We splashed several potatoes in amongst the fish, and Rolf kept adjusting the angle of the tube and volume of hair spray until we could lob a spud onto the island. "There, take that." he said triumphantly. We had apparently struck a blow for something or other.

TWENTY-THREE

ROLF DETERMINED THAT WE were obliged to make another furtive inspection of the island, not content with having shelled it.

"To see if there are any corpses with potatoes protruding from their skulls?" I inquired.

"No, that place just requires surveillance." He could neither be kidded nor insulted out of his fixation over the damn island.

"Okay," I attempted to stall, "we'll go look at it again tomorrow."

"No, we ought to check on it tonight, when it's good and dark."

"Oh, Jeez. It's hard enough to see what you're doing there in broad daylight."

"You don't have to come. I can reconnoiter by myself."

"Oh, no. I'm not going to buy another boat in the morning to go searching for you."

We set forth on the lake after midnight, when most elders had been in bed for some hours. There was no wind, no moon, and a light overcast that made it exceptionally dark. Only our anchor and bow lights provided a modicum of ambient light onto the water. Tina was nearly invisible wherever she chose to locate in the boat.

I maneuvered past the north shore of the island and then doubled back near the northwest corner, trying to assess the distance to the shore that would be nearest the trailer parked in the woods. With hand signals, Rolf kept urging me to get in closer as I throttled to a crawl and strained to make out any detail beyond the gentle lap of surface that reflected the bow light. The tops of the trees were barely visible against the sky, but at ground level all else was blacker than the inside of a cow. The white trunk of a birch tree, fallen in the lake, a frequent target of Rolf's casting, gave me a modest landmark, and I eased the boat in next to it. As we touched the bank, I called for Tina.

"Don't let her out of the boat." Too late, she was already bounding into the dark, anxiously anticipating the adventure, whatever the hell it was.

"Damn it, Rolf," I yelled, "Why did you let her go."

"Well I thought she was with you and then she launched herself like a torpedo. Ahc. Tina, come!"

She dutifully appeared off the bow as Rolf struggled to hold the boat and get a grip on the dog. More ahcs. From what I could see of his position he was getting a shoe full of water. *Serves him right.* After some cussing and thrashing, Tina was back in the boat and Rolf was leaning precariously on the bow with his feet on the fallen birch. I still had the motor idling forward, trying to hold the nose against the bank.

What occurred next was like a scene out of one of those improbable horror movies or a Marx Brothers comedy, depending on your vantage point. A brilliant, blinding beam from a spotlight suddenly split the darkness, illuminating the boat and the three of us. I yelled to Rolf to get in even as he was getting his belly over the bow, fulminating, "Sombitch! Sombitch! Sombitch!" as I began backing the boat. Although blinded by the strong beam, I was aware of objects hurling through the air and splashes next to the boat, and then heard something hit the hull.

"Get out, Fuckers!" a big booming voice shouted from behind the light. Tina barked back her defiance, adding to the general bedlem.

"What the hell was that?" I said as we got some distance from the island.

"Not too neighborly, were they," was Rolf's response.

"What hit the boat?"

"I think it was just a rock or a chunk of wood."

"Just. We're lucky they didn't take a shot at us. Damn kids."

"Those weren't kids," Rolf was quick to assert. "I saw the outline of one of them when the beam focused on you for a minute. He was big as a buffalo."

I was relieved that none of us had suffered any injury and announced as much. But Rolf was invigorated by the engagement expressing a, "We got 'em right were we want 'em now," attitude.

He wanted to go back the next day, despite our harrowing encounter. But I was adamant that we steer clear of the bedeviled place, and besides, we had promised to help Ida with some fix-up, clean-up chores.

I mowed the lawn and trimmed a hedge that had gotten out of hand while Rolf repaired a screen door hinge and checked Ida's car. He suggested that she have the tires rotated and urged her to get some diagnostic work done on the engine, his highly trained ear having detected a possible malady.

Two days later, as the "For Sale" sign went up, a half-dozen cars arrived and real estate agents from around the region acquainted themselves with the property. We noted that Deputy Lundquist's voluptuous wife was among them. She was hard not to note.

TWENTY-FOUR

WE CONTINUED TO FUSS over Hansen's, keeping the grass groomed like a golf course, because there was a steady if not heavy amount of traffic on Bankers Drive after the notices in local papers. Some were just lookers, but Ida and the various agents had a handful of appointments. And in these idyllic days of June, the lakeshore home showed off to its best.

Rolf continued to campaign for another look at the island, although he was urging a daylight mission. And I kept resisting with a variety of complaints and excuses. But we couldn't avoid fishing forever, and any venture out onto Ten Mile Lake was bound to get us closer to the now infamous island. Finally, about mid-June, on a bright sunny day with several other fishing boats in proximity, Rolf urged me to beach by the fallen birch tree so that he could scout. This time I held onto Tina, and Rolf agreed to observe carefully and return promptly. To my relief he was back aboard within a couple of minutes. The black trailer was gone.

Rolf was stumped as to our next move, and I could hardly conceal my glee. "Now we're done screwing around with the island," I proclaimed. But events would prove, yet again, that I was no prophet.

We had just refueled at the truck stop on I-94 and Highway 59 bound for Fergus Falls on one of our routine shopping trips. I had not seen the big black pickup until its rumble announced its approach from behind. The body of the truck was perched high on a modified chassis and rolled down the freeway on giant balloon tires. I noted it to Rolf who turned to look out the rear window. He said it had been at the truck stop.

The odd-looking rig continued overtaking us at a high rate of speed, the big tires causing an increasingly loud racket. I was driving about sixty-five miles per hour and eased off a bit in order to let the monster get on by us. But once abreast, the bizarre truck slowed to our speed and began edging toward us.

A pair of big ugly galoots glowered down at us from their high cab. They had masses of black hair on their heads and faces and more of it blossoming out from under white undershirts. The passenger displayed a demonic grins as the truck crowded within a few feet of us.

"What the hell?" I said, increasingly annoyed. "Those two look like a couple of wooly mammoths."

"Those are the guys from the island," Rolf said.

"Well wherever they're from they're starting a game of chicken." I applied speed to get away from them, but they kept abreast and began to edge a little ahead and closer in what resembled a rodeo steer wrestling exercise. My right tires hit the rumble strip as I fudged over, and they moved right over with us edging to within inches. Approaching a small lake right next to the freeway, the Ford shuddered and rocked dangerously as a big balloon tire rubbed my left front fender.

They're going to shove us into the lake. "Hang onto Tina!" I yelled.

I had never been in a situation like this before, but some sort of survival instinct took over in nanoseconds. I slammed on the breaks going from seventy to zero in a few feet. As our tormentors screeched to a stop in a cloud of dust, just ahead of us, half on the shoulder, I lunged around them on the left and accelerated at high speed. My Ford was usually driven no faster than seventy or seventy-five, but I soon had it wound up to eighty-five. Looking in the side mirror I was perplexed to see that the wooly mammoths were in hot pursuit and gaining. The game was not over for them.

I knew that we were approaching Exit 57, a long, gradual ramp off I-94, the back door into Fergus, and slowed slightly to let them think that they were overtaking me then, as the monster truck drew adjacent a second time, I wrenched the wheel and shot up the exit ramp, barely able to stop as I crested the 210 overpass. The narrow off ramp had denied them the option of following alongside. From the overpass we saw the big black truck thunder down I-94 on the other side of 210.

Only then did I turn to look at my passengers. Rolf was wide-eyed, his feet to the floorboards, his body tensed, clutching Tina. Oblivious to our near-death experience, Tina shattered the tension by turning and administering a big sloppy lick on his mouth. He had never provided such an opportunity and she was going to make the most of it. "Ahc. No French kissing or any other kind." As he was wiping his mouth, he added, "That was some great driving on your part."

"Best landing I ever made."

I continued down 210 to Cascade Avenue, and then it was just a few blocks to the County Court House. "We need to report this."

We arrived before the Otter Tail County government complex a bit too fast and jumped out of the Ford, hustling toward the front door. The sheriff, Jim Erlansen, and our attorney, Mark Anderson, happened to be standing together, talking on the lower step. They looked at us with some anticipation, apparently noting our agitation.

"Everything okay?" Mark asked.

"Not by a long shot," I replied. "Either we were just victims of road rage or attempted murder."

We described the event, addressing the sheriff, who started us up the steps and into his offices for a full report. Although I was still shaken, Rolf seemed in command of himself, and Tina was positively tickled, never having been in the Otter Tail County building.

"Did you get a license plate?" Apparently I had concentrated on my driving, never having been in a chase scene before, because I didn't have any answers.

Rolf took over. "Truck didn't have a plate. But we know who they are. We've seen these bozos on the island on South Ten Mile Lake, a couple of big hairy guys. We told Ed Lundquist about them a long time ago. He told us not to worry."

The sheriff got that distant, roving look of someone attempting to clear his thinking, reboot his memory.

"I'll talk to Ed. You come on in here and give a full description of these guys and the incident to one of my people. But you fellows had better stay alert. I don't like the sound of this."

The deputy took notes on everything we could remember and even went out to the truck with a camera to photograph the black scuffmarks left by the balloon tires on the left front fender. We omitted any mention of our inspection trips to the island as a possible trigger.

As we left the Court House, Rolf said, "Now we know how they drove on and off that island. It was those big tires. I guess it isn't finished after all."

I thought I detected a note of triumph in his voice, but I had a feeling of combat fatigue that hadn't surfaced since 1945.

IDA HANSEN TOLD US THAT HER FAMILY was planning one last fling at the lake. Both daughters, husbands, and grandchildren were due up the first week of July. "On Friday, the Fourth we're going to have a big picnic dinner, weather permitting, and we'd like you boys to come." We protested mildly. "No," Ida said, "you've both been so good to me and such a huge help. The kids want to thank you for doing all those things that they couldn't get here to do." I knew the daughters, Carol and Bonnie, had met their husbands and recognized a couple of the older grand kids, but they were mostly unknown to Rolf.

"Oh, and bring your vegetable shooter. It'd be great fun."

"Potato cannon," Rolf corrected.

"Whatever," Ida said. "They'll all love it since we now have such sane Fourth of Julys. The gang will go back to the Cities on Sunday, and then I need to get my car into the dealer in Fergus for the maintenance work that Rolf suggested. So, if you can follow me in on Monday and bring me back here, then give me another lift in on Tuesday morning, I'll be on my way to St. Paul."

"Absolutely," we agreed. "What about real estate showings?"

"The realtor will put his lock box on the front door so they can take care of any inspections after I leave."

TWENTY-FIVE

I had pretty much put the road rage incident behind me, but Rolf brooded about it. We had survived, the police were informed, and I was convinced that we had seen the last of them. "Just a pair of ignorant bullies acting out their aggression," was my way of trying to lay it to rest.

"There's more to it than that," Rolf insisted.

"You're always seeing plots. Let's go to the Fourth of July celebration. I can hear the Hansen kids already."

Indeed, as we pulled into the driveway, the yard was alive with people, and the grills were smoking. Tom and Keith, the sons-in-law, were firing the charcoal while six cousins ranging from twenty-year-old Bart to five-year-old Kurt were frolicking between the house and the lake. Each daughter had three children, and they were equally divided, three boys and three girls, all handsome and beautiful. Tina was soon among them breaking up the girl's game of croquet by retrieving a rolling ball and returning it to me. Bonnie greeted us and reintroduced the two husbands I had only met briefly. They had not met Rolf, and he was his usual reserved self until Keith pulled a cold beer from an icy bucket and thrust it into his hand. Carol and Ida soon appeared from the house with dishes of food for an already overflowing buffet table on the deck.

"Sit down and enjoy your beers," Ida directed. "We'll eat when you're hungry. But first Rolf, show the kids your cannon."

Rolf did his version of, "Aw, shucks," and went back to the truck for the mortar and ammo.

I sat on the deck with a beer and a hand on Tina's collar. "Get the kids up from the lake. They're in the line of fire." The warning was unnecessary as they were drawn to Rolf's contraption like moths to a flame. He gave the assembled crowd a briefing on the potato cannon and made some crew assignments. Bart went to the shoreline to keep an eye out for boaters. The fathers were told to keep the crowd back and watch for the outgoing rounds. Thirteen-year-old Joe was assigned to drop the potatoes down the tube. The girls had stepped back by their mothers, showing indifference to what they correctly gauged as an exercise in male nonsense. Rolf had omitted little Kurt who hung back by his grandmother slightly afraid yet a bit miffed at being on the sidelines. I noticed that his lower lip was growing.

The first yell of "Fire in the hole!" and the attendant *FONG* was followed by a satisfying splash about ten feet offshore. The crowd hooted and cheered except for five-year-old Kurt who seemed impressed but still pissed. Rolf gave each of the boys and their dads a turn at the firing mechanism. With the next several shots little Kurt's lower lip got bigger. I decided to intervene.

"Rolf, juggle your crew a bit. Kurt here needs to learn the manly art of potato mortaring."

A lifetime without children had made him awkward with small ones, and his stern countenance kept Kurt at bay. Rolf cracked a smiled and came over to the young boy, and I believe at that moment he exhibited parenting that had been dormant for fifty years. "I got a bad knee. I could use some help over there at the cannon."

Kurt had backed a few steps until he was up against his grandmother. "What happened to your knee," he asked.

"Old pirate wound," Rolf said with customary brevity.

Kurt eyed him balefully and looked at Ida. She smiled and gave him a "go ahead" nod. He looked Rolf in the eye and said, "Can I yell?"

Rolf smiled as much as he ever did and said, "You get to pull the trigger and yell 'Fire in the hole!'"

Kurt turned to Ida and said, "Oh, boy, fire in de hole." Then he took Rolf's hand and they advanced on the cannon as the adult ladies stifled laughs.

The two of them squatting by the base of the mortar made a great picture, which Bonnie snapped: the child and the descendant of Einar the Eviscerator. When Rolf had his troops ready, and Bart had waved that the coast was clear, little Kurt pulled the trigger and yelled in his best big boy voice, "Fire in de hole!" *FONG* went the gun, and another potato arched on to the lake amid a chorus of cheers. Kurt jumped up and down then hugged Rolf around the knees. I thought the old boy might cry. It was a toss up as to which one had gotten more profound joy out of the moment.

There were more mortar shots, the granddaughters even getting in on the crew action, until we ran out of potatoes and Ida said it was time to eat. As we gathered around the picnic tables, Kurt scrambled next to Rolf and they struck up a conversation about pirating. Bonnie sat next to Kurt and the three granddaughters all grabbed seats opposite Rolf, seemingly intrigued by the austere old goat with the childish cannon that shot potatoes.

"Walf was a piwate," Kurt informed his mother with his slight lisp.

"Really!" Bonnie had never known a real live pirate. "Ask him if he can give us some authentic pirate talk."

"Can you talk piwate?" Kurt asked his dinner companion. "My mom wants to know."

Rolf rose to the occasion. "Ahrg, matey. Shiver your timbers and blast your scuppers." He hesitated for inspiration. "Maybe after supper we'll make your mom walk the plank. Off the dock that is, into the lake." The girls rolled their eyes at such silliness, but Kurt beamed.

"Wow!" Kurt exclaimed, then considered for a moment. "How about my sista Kate instead of my Mom?"

Bonnie guffawed as ten-year-old Kate said, "You little creep."

Aware of the direction of the conversation at the other table, I called over to Rolf. "If you're causing trouble over there, we might have to send you home."

"Oh, God. Don't send him away," Ida said. "He's more fun than a barrel of monkeys."

There were burgers, hot dogs, brats, potato salad (two kinds), Jell-O salad, melon chunks, corn on the cob, and beer to wash it all down. And after that they asked who wanted dessert. Only the kids had any room left, having had sufficient exercise to accommodate the final course. The adults, pleasantly stuffed, just rested and marveled that the youngsters and Tina were back at various recreational pursuits. Periodically you could hear someone at a distance saying, "Fire in de hole," or "Grama, do you want to walk the plank? It might cool you off."

It had been a grand gathering, and as the sun began to lower, Tina, Rolf, and I expressed out gratitude for a memorable day. We had been taken into the bosom of this marvelous family and shared their affectionate attachment. For inveterate bachelors it had been a rare experience.

Of course, nothing would do but Ida loaded us with left over food. "No point in putting it in the frig. I won't be here to eat it." So we were compelled to carry off booty just like a band of pirates would.

"Goobye, Walf!" echoed in our ears as we started down the road. I believe I saw a tear in the corner of the old boy's eye as he waved back to little Kurt.

Despite being gorged on Ida's food and tired from the day's activities, I convinced Rolf to sit on the deck for a time. There was still the Ten Mile Lake boat parade and the fireworks display at the resort. We didn't have a direct view of the resort, but could see the high bursts over the intruding trees.

The boat parade, a procession of fishing and pontoon boats was a raucous affair where shore-based parties moved onto the water, and inebriated skippers maneuvered their vessels into a sort of ragged line that followed the shoreline from south to north. In some cases boats merged with neighbors and loud boardings took place, but there seemed to be no plank walking or keel hauling activity. The exercise involved no great feats of seamanship yet, in the spirit of things, dock sitters, mostly grandparents cheered noisily as the flotilla passed. It was Ten Mile Lake's burlesque of New York's Maritime Day parade. As soon as it was dark the boaters all hovered at the north end of the lake to position themselves near the barrage of fireworks that lofted up from the road near the resort. It seemed inevitable that an errant rocket or Roman candle might set off a boat's gas tank. Perhaps that latent danger was part of what the crowd enjoyed on a Fourth of July evening.

The dusk drifted into darkness, and we watched as boat lights bobbed on the water and rockets blossomed in the air. Eventually the hectic activity subsided and we were left with only the sound of an occasional fish slapping the water and Tina, between us, snoring and occasionally farting.

"What did she get into?"

"Wieners, I saw Kurt feeding them to her," Rolf explained. "She had a good time too."

I agreed. "I haven't had this much fun since we fed my baby brother to the hogs."

Rolf sighed thoughtfully, and after a time said, "How much we've missed."

TWENTY-SIX

MONDAY MORNING I FOLLOWED Ida into town to her car dealership then returned her to the lake. We tried to talk her into a dinner at the Steak House but she begged off. Too much packing and last-minute cleaning to do, she insisted. I agreed to pick her up early next morning so that she could retrieve her car from Fergus Falls.

It was cloudy and raining lightly that next morning as I parked in Hansen's driveway. The weather magnified my depression as I looked at the FOR SALE sign and pondered the void that Ida's moving would have on my life. Paul and Ida Hansen had gone out of their way to introduce themselves the day I first bought my cabin. I had arrived here as a grumpy old curmudgeon and their infectious charm had helped transform me or at least prevent the county certifying me as a resident nut case.

How many good times had I spent in their fine home? And this would be the end of it, Paul gone these few months and Ida about to leave. I focused on the real estate dealer's lock box on the front door and pondered what sort of people might live here in the future: old, young, kids. It was a large split level with an oversized attached garage and a $450,000 asking price, so the next owners wouldn't be any band of gypsies. But they couldn't possibly compare to the Hansens. Here I was worrying about how unknown neighbors might intrude on my insular life. *How must Ida feel? By the way, where was she?* No wave from a window. No sign of her.

I had waited several minutes when I decided to take the umbrella from behind the seat, do the gallant thing and go to the door to escort her out. I knocked then rang the bell. No answer. Perhaps she had overslept. I rang again, and still no response. Maybe she was on the deck but that seemed unlikely with the rain.

Tramping around the north side of the house that faced my place, I walked to the west side and up the two-tiered deck. What fun we had all had here just days before. The sliding glass doors afforded a view of their spacious great room and I could see through to the kitchen. No sign of Ida and seemingly no lights. The door was locked, so after tapping for a bit I headed to the attached garage on the south side.

The door on the lake was unlocked and I crossed the large empty garage to a door that provided access to the house. It was dark in the garage, and I groped for the steel fire door. To my surprise it was slightly ajar. Easing it open I called to Ida as I ascended the stairs that put me in the kitchen. There was still no answer, so I kept on calling. She must have overslept, and I worried that I would scare her to death. But when the only sound in the house was my own voice I began to have different concerns.

What was that strange smell? I'd smelled it before, a long repressed memory of an odor that momentarily summoned the scene as I took the pilot's seat in our wounded B-24.

Timidly, I eased toward the hall that led to the bedrooms. Because of the clouds it was still dim, and as I called out Ida's name I wondered how such a fine housekeeper could have left a pile of clothing in the hallway. As I got a step or two closer I realized that the pile had form. It was Ida face down. And as I hurried near, it looked like she had tipped over a bucket of paint where she seemed to have fallen.

"My God, Ida, what happened?"

I went down on one knee and placed a hand on her shoulder, noting that she was still in her nightgown. And then that odor from 1945 assaulted my senses again. *Why was her hair matted in the paint?*

She was facing the wall and as I raised her head and turned her face toward me I saw the gash below her chin to the left ear. That beautiful smile had vanished and she stared at me through half open eyes. Her face was white, like a grotesque mask of the lovely lady I had known.

"Mother of God," I lowered her and reared back against the opposite wall. My head swam. Dear Ida was dead and cold, lying in a puddle of her own congealing blood, her throat cut.

I leaped to the phone and called 911. It was answered in the sheriff's office in Fergus Falls, and I asked for an ambulance, realizing that it was hopeless but I couldn't bring myself to say she had been murdered, but said that it looked like an assault. As I hung up the phone I noted things that had eluded me before: the gun cabinet in the great room was open and empty, and Ida's purse was on the dining room table, its contents seemingly dumped there. Before I could ponder the obvious meaning, I returned to Ida, hoping for a miracle. Perhaps I had been too hasty. I snapped on a hall light and felt for a heartbeat or a breath. There was nothing to indicate the vibrancy of life in her cold body

Beginning to feel nauseous, I stumbled to the front door and could hear a siren as I stepped out. Within a minute a State Highway Patrol car came rocketing in from the east onto Bankers Drive. The trooper had apparently been on I-94 near the Dalton exit when the call went out.

As we entered the house, he asked about the situation and who I was, then told me to please wait within sight of him while he checked Ida, stating that I should touch nothing. While I hovered in the kitchen, a sheriff's car pulled into the driveway while the trooper confirmed that she was dead. "Please step outside and get in the back of my car if you will." As I numbly obliged him, Deputy Ed Lundquist was coming up the steps. The officers conferred briefly while I began to wretch next to the garage.

I don't know if I sat in the back of the squad car for fifteen minutes or fifty, but there was a tap on the window and I looked up to see a puzzled Rolf with Tina in tow. The driveway now held an ambulance and another pair of sheriff's cruisers.

"What the hell's going on?" Rolf asked, his face a mask of concern. "I took Tina out for a pee and saw all this traffic."

"Oh, God, Rolf. It's Ida. I think she's been murdered."

He started for the Hansen house as I began to exit the squad car. "Hold up there you two," Ed Lundquist yelled from the doorway. "You both have some heavy explaining to do. Odell, you stay where you are, and you," he pointed to Rolf, "get in the back of my car."

Rolf didn't hesitate for a minute as he headed toward Hansen's door. Lundquist put a hand on his arm and Rolf squared away as if to put up a scrap. "Don't be a dumb ass," he said to Lundquist.

"Now don't you give me any trouble," Ed said, "You two were awful close to this."

Standing next to the highway patrol car, I urged Rolf to back off. "I can see their point. This is a crime scene, and believe me, you can't do anything for Ida." Reluctantly we both followed orders, but I left the door of the trooper's car open so that Tina could sit next to me.

The ambulance left but the procession of official vehicles continued to swell with the arrival of two more from the county, a van from the County Coroner and Sheriff Jim Erlansen with another plain clothes deputy. They all went inside for a time, and then Erlansen came out to us. "Mike, did you touch anything in there?"

"Hell, I touched everything. And we were both here just a few days ago for the Fourth."

"Why were you there this morning and how did you gain access?"

I explained the plan to give Ida a ride to town. Then on reflection mentioned the inner garage door being ajar.

"Okay, Mike, you and Rolf go on home, but promise me you'll stay there until my investigator can take your complete statements."

"It won't be Lundquist will it?" Rolf asked.

"No," the sheriff said with a quizzical look, "his name is Bill Berg."

We readily agreed and plodded down the road. I was in a daze and Rolf looked as if he might blow a gasket. "We should have protected her," he said.

"Rolf, I feel as bad as you do, but how were we to know? What could we have done differently?"

"That's just it. We didn't do anything. We failed her." If falling on my sword at that point might have brought Ida back I would gladly have done it.

For an hour we sat dumbly, neither of us believing what had happened, until the sheriff's investigator arrived. Rolf was prepared to be contentious until Berg explained that we had to be interviewed because we were critical to solving the crime. After some preliminary questions, he asked if he could search the house and garage. We readily agreed and again, sat brooding and stewing while he completed the task. Returning to us he asked, "Do either of you own a fish knife, one that could be used for gutting and or filleting?"

The answer was yes from both of us, and we led him to those items in our kitchen and our tackle boxes. "I'll need to take these for examination."

"Fine," we agreed grimly, understanding that they suspected such a knife as the possible murder weapon.

Finally, he asked us to accompany him back to Hansen's. We noticed that the coroner's van had left but a medium-sized RV had arrived from the state crime lab, Bureau of Criminal Apprehension. Police officers seemed to be everywhere, searching the grounds and the house.

First of all, Deputy Berg asked me to walk through the route I had taken that morning from arrival until I found the body and called 911. I did this while Rolf and Tina sat on the deck or trod the property. Tina wagged her tail at every cop, but Rolf was talking to himself and looked like he might have a nervous breakdown. His anguish was so apparent that Berg asked me about it. "He has no family, and in a very short period of time had become very attached to the Hansens. He . . . we feel responsible to a degree."

As we entered through the house I was shown the broken doorframe in the garage where the door had been pried open. I had not seen it in the dim light earlier. Berg also said that the coroner estimated the death had taken place about 2:00 or 3:00 a.m.

After a trip to the BCA vehicle for fingerprinting, Rolf and I emerged to find Sheriff Erlansen waiting. "Why did this happen, Sheriff?"

"For guns, a marketable commodity, and cash if they stumble across any. They must have thought that the house was empty with the FOR SALE sign, real estate ads in the paper, the lock box. And the garage was empty. They didn't expect to confront anyone, but she saw them."

"And the dirty sombitches just killed her," Rolf said with great emotion.

"I'm afraid so. With a very sharp, pointed knife from the looks of the wound. We need to keep your knives for some forensic testing, but I know you boys didn't do this. Go get some new knives."

"And if we find the killers before you do, we'll carve their hearts out," Rolf said with rage in his voice and demeanor.

"Don't count us out, Mr. Holt. We'll work like demons to apprehend the killer or killers. We have our resources, and we are as angered by a crime like this as you are. We live here too."

Rolf calmed a bit, and we both nodded.

"Do you know the next of kin, Mike?"

"Yes. Oh, God. We were with all of them just a few days ago."

The sheriff held up a list of names and phone numbers. "These were next to a telephone in the kitchen—mostly numbers in the Cities. Can you help us identify family names and numbers?"

"These are her daughters," I pointed and gave the sheriff a baleful look.

"Well, they have to be notified. It might be slightly easier—less shock—on them if it was a familiar voice."

"I'm sure you're right. But I'd rather have both legs broken than have to make that call."

It was getting toward noon and Ida would have been pulling into the Twin Cities about this time. "I'd better bite the bullet." I called Carol first and got an answering machine, then dialed Bonnie. It was a grim task that left her stunned and me in tears.

"Oh, Lord, that was the toughest thing I've ever had to do."

Rolf put an arm on my shoulder. "I'm proud of you. I couldn't do it."

TWENTY-SEVEN

THAT EVENING, AS WE SAT IN dumb silence, the phone rang, causing us to jump. It was Bonnie's husband, Keith Hall. "Mike, we are finally surfacing here and are beginning to wonder about funeral arrangements. Where is . . ." he hesitated, "Ida now?"

"The coroner took her, and I don't know what that means except that I'm sure it's part of the investigation. And believe me they are being thorough."

"Could you find out for us what they have in mind? When we might have her?"

"I'll call the county sheriff right now, but doubt that I'll get an answer until morning."

"When you find out, call me on my cell phone." I was glad to have that number, as I didn't think I could handle another emotional conversation with Bonnie. He asked a few more questions until he couldn't bear to hear any more details, and I couldn't bear to go on.

Rolf and I sat up until all hours, saying little, both of us too full of anger and bitterness to sleep. Rolf kept muttering that we were barely 100 yards away and still she died alone. No response was adequate. No excuse suitable.

I had developed a whopper of a headache and long after midnight took some Tylenol and an Ambien washed down with considerable Scotch. The combination should have rendered me senseless, still I only slept fitfully amid fearful visions of Ida as I had lifted her head and turned her waxy face toward me.

At eight sharp, Wednesday morning, I called Sheriff Erlansen. He said that Bill Berg, his investigator would be out our way with a team of people shortly, would like to see us again, and would answer any questions. Would we please stay put?

Several deputies returned at the Hansen house while Berg came to our cabin. Tina barked a warning when he knocked on our door, then as he sat at our kitchen table, wanted to be his buddy, putting her head in his lap and giving him her, "Uh, Uh," routine. I poured coffee for the three of us. It helped to chase away the cobwebs but not the gloom.

First he advised us that the coroner would be ready to release the body by late Friday and gave us the number of a local funeral director. I immediately called Keith Hall to advise him of these facts and asked that he let us know when and where services would be conducted.

Bill Berg was wrapped around his coffee mug and stared at the rising steam for some time. "First of all, let me give you a summary of what we have so far. You were right, finger prints of you two were evident in several places, mostly yours, Mike." We both stiffened. "But," he hastened to add; "you are not considered a suspect by Sheriff Erlansen."

"Somebody does consider me a knife murderer?"

"There are those in the department who consider you a prime suspect. I'm not one of them."

"There are a number of prints that can't be identified." Berg went on, "Some belonged to Tom Fellows."

"Yes, that's one of Ida's sons-in-law. He was just there for a long weekend. The other son-in-law is Keith Hall, the guy I just called. But why would you find a record of Tom's prints?"

"It was in the government data base. Possibly he was in the military?"

"Yes, he was, several years in the Army, and I can guarantee you he would not sneak up here to steal Paul's guns and kill his wife's mother. He is a sterling guy and has been a member of the family for over twenty years. Hell, Ida would probably have given Paul's guns to Keith and Tom when she sold and moved."

Berg made some notes. "Just for the record, we'll have the St. Paul police check on his whereabouts the night of the murder. We don't have much else to go on in the way of hard evidence. The killer may have been wearing gloves. But we do have a couple of partial shoe prints in the blood, and we have a funny looking tire track in the yard next door"

Rolf, who had been sitting silently, emitted an "Ahc!" as if to say *I knew it.*

Deputy Berg glanced at him for a bit but stayed on focus. "I need to see the shoes that both of you might have, if you'll direct me to your closets and then let me check those you are wearing."

We led him to our modest shoe inventory and then showed him what we had on. "I was wearing these tennis shoes when I found Ida," I volunteered, pulling off both New Balance shoes for inspection.

"Okay. That's one of the profiles we found in the blood. Show me how you approached her body." I demonstrated how I knelt next to her on my right knee with my left foot in the center of the hall.

"Right, figured that was you, a size nine. There was another partial big shoe or boot print almost under her head. And we don't know who belongs to that, big though, probably a size twelve." Again Rolf belched up an involuntary, "Ahc!"

Deputy Berg eyed Rolf and said, "Now is there anything else you guys want to tell me? Any strange activities around here?"

Rolf and I exchanged momentary glances before he jumped into the discussion. "That island, right over there," he pointed. "Weird things are happening out there. We've seen lights at night, and in the daytime we scouted and found a big enclosed cargo trailer out there. Made no sense to us that it should be in a place like that. So we went back several times and we saw these two bozos. A few nights ago we were fishing and we put ashore there and they put a light on us, cussed us, and threw things at us. After that, we checked again in daylight and the trailer was gone. Shortly after that these same two goons tried to run us off Highway 94." It was the longest speech I had heard from Rolf since he had told me his war stories.

Berg had listened intently, making notes. "I read that road-rage report. The sheriff remembered it." He hesitated. "And you're sure that the two from the island were the same as the pair in the Highway 94 incident." We both nodded agreement.

"And the truck they were driving, with those big balloon tires, is the only thing that could have driven that trailer over the island causeway," I said, putting a map of South Ten Mile Lake on the table and pointing to the narrow isthmus.

"And you saw no license plates on either the truck or the trailer?"

Again Rolf responded for both of us: "We sure looked, but there were no plates."

I poured some more coffee in each cup as Bill Berg made a steeple with his hands and put the two index fingers to his lips. His solitary contemplation was broken when Rolf said, "We told Deputy Lundquist about our suspicion that something was happening on that island."

"And what did he say?"

"He treated us like a couple of old busybodies," I answered. "Told us not to trespass."

Berg began to pull his notes together. "Do you intend to go to funeral services for Mrs. Hansen?"

"You bet," Rolf replied as I nodded my agreement.

I was dissatisfied with the outcome of the meeting. "Do you know something about these guys?"

Berg chose his words carefully. "No. But there is a gang doing break-ins in an area of several counties around here and stealing firearms primarily. Presumably they sell them at out-of-state gun shows. They are very sly, and have never gone into an occupied residence. They leave no prints and seem to vanish into thin air. They may even be operating from just across the Dakota border. Let me know when you leave and call me when you return." He hesitated at the door and then turned back. "I don't want to frighten you, but keep your eyes open."

Rolf and I glanced at each other, and he gave a derisive, "Ahc! We both should have died fifty years ago. We've known danger before."

I added, "We'll circle the wagons."

The detective gave Tina a departing ear scratch. "And keep your home security system well fed. A dog's alert senses are the ultimate crime fighter."

THE THREE OF US LEFT BEFORE DAWN for Ida's funeral in St. Paul. It had been just one week since her brutal murder. Rolf and I were silent and reflective not relishing a meeting with the Hansen family but determined to pay our respects. Tina had been jolly and alert at first, sitting up between, us looking out the window, sight seeing. But after an hour or so she lay down, butt against me and head against Rolf. Now and then Rolf would absentmindedly stroke her, and Tina would emit a soft rumble.

There was to be no wake, just a memorial mass at Nativity church between the Highland and Groveland neighborhoods. The church was packed, but this was nothing like Paul's funeral. No celebration of life, for a life had been cruelly taken. This was a stark, senseless tragedy. The priest had a rotten job but made an attempt at offering some peace of mind. He blathered on about Ida's reward. But the bowed heads and flowing tears showed that there was scant little relief engendered by the sermon. He spoke of how in his mercy God had brought Ida home to heaven, and I couldn't help but wonder if that was so why God hadn't in his infinite mercy seen fit to spare her. I muttered my silent Hail Marys for her, tuning out the priest.

The internment was to be private. How much pain could one family bear? So the Hansen daughters, their husbands and children stood like soldiers on the steps of Nativity on Stanford Avenue and greeted people as the throng filed from the church. As nearly as I could tell there were none of the usual expressions of sympathy. What could you say that would afford any sense of relief? By the time I got to Carol and Bonnie, their beautiful faces distorted and eyes reddened by profound sorrow, my Irish emotions had overwhelmed me, and I was of no comfort. I merely hugged them as we wept. There were no words adequate for our shared grief.

Rolf was his usual stoic self and grim as a park statue, his simmering rage preventing him from weeping until little Kurt spotted him, waved and said, "Hi, Walf." Rolf extended his hand for a shake but a smiling Kurt put up both of his arms. Not fully understanding the sadness that seemed to engulf the gathering of adults, the five-year-old wanted a hug from his favorite pirate. Rolf went down on one knee and embraced the child, and as he rose I saw the tears coursing down his weathered face.

Before we could retreat to the truck, Tom Fellows sought us out in the crowd and gave us each a crushing handshake. "We all appreciate what you've gone through and want to thank you for being her friend and coming here."

Before I could respond Rolf said, "Thank us? Hell, you ought to shoot us. As close as we were, we couldn't protect her."

"No, don't blame yourselves for this. I don't agree with the pastor that it was part of some divine plan, but there are some things you can't guard against."

He hesitated for just a moment, "There are a lot of things to be considered about the lake place, but not right now. Please keep an eye on it and we'll talk later."

"We bungled the job last time," Rolf quickly interjected, as Tom shook his head dismissively.

"Of course we will," I responded, "and we'll help any way we can."

After Tina had a pee, we started back up I-94, the return trip spent largely in sober silence. By the time we reached the cabin, three hours later, I had another hammering headache.

TWENTY-EIGHT

A T 8:00 A.M. THE NEXT MORNING I called Deputy Berg to advise him that we were back and ask if there were any new developments. "There might be something soon, but I'm not at liberty to discuss it: ongoing investigation and all that. But I think we're getting close."

I said I understood but didn't really. Again he cautioned us to stay alert.

"I'll sleep with one eye open," as my dad used to say.

I relayed Berg's comment that they were getting closer. Rolf snarled, "Only counts in horseshoes and hand grenades."

It was warm that day, so we sat out on the deck, too long lost in our thoughts and drinking too much. Tina had slept most of the way home and was busier than a one-armed paperhanger trying to get rid of chipmunks that had flourished during our absence. Gone for a day, and the little critters apparently thought we had moved out for good. She watched them from the deck and then scurried down the steps to send them diving into their new holes. They had judged the distance and pursuit perfectly, always jumping into their holes at just the last minute. Tina would insert her big black muzzle into the void right up to her eyes and inhale deeply, as if she might vacuum one to the surface. Alas, the rodents stayed deep in their warrens, and after a loud nose snort resembling a small explosion, Tina would return to her observation post on the deck. It was a modest but welcome diversion from our unremitting gloom.

WE'VE GOT TO START DOING SOMETHING, anything," I said the next morning over my runny, insufficiently scrambled eggs. "I guess I could begin by doing the eggs right. And the toast is overdone. I'm just not able to concentrate."

Nodding in agreement with everything Rolf suggested, "Let's do our yard work, then go fishing. You need to focus when you're doing that sort of stuff."

So we mowed the hell out of four yards then drove over to check our duck slough. Cornfields surrounded it this summer and the corn was lush and already about six feet tall. The water level was where it should be and puddle ducks bobbed on the surface with their broods following. The adults were flightless now, in the molting stage. Then we drove into Dalton for some minnows. Busy, busy, busy.

A subsequent tour of our favorite spots on South Ten Mile Lake allowed us to exercise our fishing skills. I avoided the evil island and Rolf seemed content to forego any new scouting expeditions. While I trolled for walleye pike with live bait, Rolf threw out everything in his tackle box at whatever finny critter might be foolish enough to get in our wake. I caught a couple of medium walleye keepers, and he uncharacteristically snagged two tree branches and several large underwater weeds. "So much for concentrating," I chided.

We had just turned off the trolling motor and were about to engage the main outboard when we saw the helicopter approaching from the northwest, its rotor *whump-whumping*. The aircraft that I judged to be a Huey, was unmarked and painted matte black. It came across the lake at about 1,000 feet going southeast and continued across the island then made a wide swing to the east, did a 180-degree turn over Highway 37 and came back across the lake going due west.

"What was that all about?" I asked. Rolf shook his head as he gazed after the departing helicopter. The chopper bore no markings, and we had never seen it before.

Forgetting the anomaly of the mysterious chopper, we filleted the fish and had them for dinner with some corn on the cob that must have been grown somewhere else. There were still side dishes in the frig from Hansen's Fourth of July party, the sight of which renewed our depression. As we cleaned up, I dumped the remainder and put the dishes in the washer.

Sitting on the deck at sunset, I sipped my Oban while Rolf chugged his beer. "We've got to get over this funk, Rolf. It isn't going to bring back Ida or solve anything."

Rolf remained silent for so long that I thought possibly he was agreeing. But then he said matter-of-fact in a low gravely voice, "Unfinished business."

I understood. We couldn't just wish it to go away. It was a wound that begged attention, a cure, or at least cauterizing. Khayyam's words drifted into my consciousness:

There was a door to which I found no key,
There was a veil past which I could not see.

We went to bed later than usual, after the late evening news, but I couldn't even doze. Ida's lifeless, shocked stare and the horrible gash along her neck kept intruding like a dream, although I was wide awake. Perhaps another noggin of scotch and some reading would work like an eraser on my memory, so I got up and returned to the great room. Good old Tina followed and was soon snoring at my feet. When the book began to slip from my hand, I judged that I might sleep. Tina grunted as she got up and dutifully followed me, I flopped on the bed, and she curled up on her mattress next to me.

The night was so calm that I could hear an occasional wave lap on the shore. I tried counting the seconds between waves, a variation on sheep. Then I determined to recollect my earliest days as a child, striving to erase Ida's murder from my mind.

It seemed that I was still awake, but in fact I had been transported back to Trinity parochial school in the seventh grade where I was dozing at my desk. Something I did quite a lot. I held a geography book with my right arm shielding my head as I laid it on the desk and looked toward the left. Mary Moriarty was in the seat next to me and turned toward me. A top student, she was diligently reading her geography. Her knees were apart and her skirt had hitched up a notch so that I had a partial view of her inner thighs. They vanished into a dark cavern the recess of which I had, of course, never investigated, but was rumored by older boys to be a place of erotic delight. It was a forbidden zone, therefore a place of addictive attraction.

Suddenly, I was aware of a shadow hovering over me. There was Sister Claudine like a giant avenging penguin standing between us and glaring down. "Mary! Straighten up and put your legs together!" Her knees clicked like colliding billiard balls. Then Sister's burning gaze fixed me like a lance. "And you, Michael Odell! What do you think you are doing?"

"Nothing, s'tir, " I stammered as I jerked myself upright and faced forward, hoping to find refuge in a map of Siberia.

She continued glaring at me, and I wondered if perhaps it was like this at the medieval inquisitions. "An idle mind is the devil's workshop," she intoned.

"Yes, s'tir."

"I will expect to see you going into the confessional tomorrow."

I gulped and studied my book with what I thought was maximum fervor. What sort of a penance could I possibly receive when I told Father Moore that I was looking up a girl's skirt, probably a whole rosary, maybe two, one for each thigh?

Oh, God, but us thirteen-year-olds sinned a lot. Contrition and penance our constant companions. Surely the devil had his sights on me. I even thought I could hear his virulent rumble. No, it was Tina's low growl that chased my dreams.

It was pitch black, but lying on my side I could see her profile, still on her mattress but with head up and ears cocked outward, on high Labrador alert.

My head still on the pillow, I could also see my night clock showing 4:46 a.m. as I detected a wind chime. But the lake was calm, no lapping of water on the shore. There was the wind chime again. *What the hell. I don't have a wind chime!* It sounded more like breaking glass.

As I rose slowly, Tina got to her feet. Even in the dark I could see that her body was tensed, like she was when scrutinizing the activities of the chipmunks. "Stay," I said in a low voice as I swung my legs to the floor and my feet groped their way into slippers. If there was broken glass somewhere I didn't want either of us walking in it. But what could have broken? Was it foraging raccoons from the woods across the road?

I eased the door to the bedroom shut just as Tina tried to squeeze past. "No, stay!" Over my left shoulder I could see that Rolf's door was open to his darkened room, as was the door to the bathroom just in front of me. To my right, down the hallway toward the main part of the house, the dim profile of things emerged from the small nightlight we always left in the kitchen. As I proceeded slowly down the hall, there was a thump behind me. Tina had butted her head on the bedroom door or smacked it with a paw.

Reaching the end of the hall, I sensed rather than saw or heard something at the corner of the wall and turned slightly left as I stepped into the great room. The blow that arced its way toward me caught me on both arms and the stomach. It was not deadly but sufficient to knock some wind out of me and drop me to the floor like a felled tree. I grunted more than yelled as I rolled onto my back and instinctively pulled my arms and legs up for protection.

I got an instant snapshot of the two woolly mammoths of island and road-rage fame, one standing just inside the back door and the other, my assailant, stepping toward me with a baseball bat. God but they were big and ugly. Both had dark, penetrating eyes, thick black eyebrows and hair sticking out from under grungy baseball caps and greasy undershirts. They looked like a couple of filthy, unmade beds. The one in the doorway was huge, well over six feet and near 300 pounds, but the near one was even bigger and more menacing as he advanced toward me, "I'm gon beat the shit out of you, old man."

Well I didn't think they had come for coffee.

The goon in the doorway smiled in moronic ecstasy at the prospect of seeing me pummeled, and the guy with the bat had the deranged intensity of one who was certifiably nuts. I was still gasping for a full breath when he began raising the bat very deliberately. He had about gotten it to maximum height over my still helpless form, rotating the cudgel as he contemplated his clubbing technique, when I heard a double click of metal from down the hall. It was vaguely familiar, a sound distantly recorded in my long-term memory: the cocking and chambering of a Colt .45 Model 1911 automatic pistol.

The report of that venerable old weapon, in the confines of the hall, resounded like a battleship's main battery. The nearest giant bozo went down heavily in increments, like a sack full of doorknobs, landing alongside me. He lay there stunned while the village idiot, now a few feet into the kitchen, stopped and stared open mouthed, uncomprehending.

"There's a second one, Rolf!" I managed to say, finally pulling myself together. The body on the floor began a low moan, Tina began a ferocious barking, and the big dummy in the kitchen started backing toward the door as he reached unsteadily for a pistol in a left hip holster.

Rolf rounded the corner looking like Thor stalking off his longship but with a Colt in front of him instead of a battleaxe. The criminal accomplice was retreating down the steps faster than I thought a man that large could move, all the while sort of whining, "Oh, Kenny, oh, Kenny!" apparently for his fallen comrade.

Rolf reached the door, and walking barefoot across the broken glass with apparent disdain, snapped on our yard light, swung the storm door, and let fly with another shot. I heard a yell from outside as Rolf calmly turned to me and nodded toward the wounded lout on the floor, "Get his weapons. I have to go deal with the other one."

The intruder on the kitchen floor was now groaning more loudly and flailing with both arms and feet as a wound on his back just below the left shoulder blade blossomed red. He was in no position to resist as I stripped his waist of holstered pistol and a knife.

In the excitement of the moment, I had largely forgotten my own pain, although it wasn't everyday I got walloped with a Louisville Slugger. Since my attacker was clearly incapable of further skullduggery, I went to the back door to look out on the yard. Rolf was disarming the other malcontent who seemed to have a burgeoning wound in his right hip, butt to be more precise, and was yelling, "Don't kill me! Don't kill me!" In the driveway was an unfamiliar beat-up pickup.

Rolf stood over him and said, "No. I'm just going to shoot you full of holes and make you suffer like Ida Hansen did."

"No. No. I never. Please, it weren't me. It were Kenny who done her."

"Who's Kenny?" Rolf said, now poking the .45 into his crotch.

The downed man, more terrified than ever, almost screamed, "In there, he's my brother. He done it. He had to. She saw him." Then as Rolf backed off a bit, the wounded man said, almost as justification for murder, "She weren't supposed to be there."

"And who might you be, you miserable excuse for a human?"

"I'm Billy Generaux. Please don't hurt me anymore, mister."

Suddenly a set of headlights lunged into the yard from Bankers Drive. It was a squad car, and I assumed some neighbor must have heard the shooting and called the sheriff.

Deputy Ed Lundquist, alone in the cruiser, stepped from behind the wheel and strode toward Rolf and the downed Billy Generaux. "Okay, I'll take charge. Put that gun on the ground, now old timer." It was his standard patronizing tone and Rolf greeted him by standing and leveling the Colt .45 at him.

"Thanks for dropping by, deputy. Now drop *your* gun belt." Lundquist kept on coming, and I wasn't sure I had heard right through the whimpering and the distant barking.

"Rolf," I called from the deck, "for God sake!"

Ed slowed his pace, but his hand began to shift toward the holstered pistol on his right hip. "Now, see here. I'm the law, and you drop that weapon before somebody gets hurt."

"We've already hurt everyone but you, and I'd be happy to remedy that," Rolf said unflinching.

Ed slowed his pace and his hand hesitated, but his mouth was in high gear, "God damnit, old shit, do as I say! Drop that gun!" His head shifted slightly toward me. "Odell, you drop the weapon you're holding too, and get down here and deal with this old fool of yours."

I was too astounded at the scene to move but said plaintively, "Rolf?" My last violent confrontation had been a food fight with my ex-wife forty years ago and I wasn't programmed for anything like this.

"Stay there, Mike. The Sombitch would like to get us side by side for a double execution."

"God damn old fool!" Ed shouted and his hand went to the butt of his gun.

Rolf lowered the angle of the .45 just slightly and sent a booming round into the dirt between Ed's feet. Deputy Lundquist crow hopped while emitting an unmanly scream, then froze in place, his right hand going to full-staff. Despite his display of fear, Ed still railed at Rolf. "That did it. You damn near hit me. Now you're in deep trouble with the law, and I demand that you drop that gun! Hell, you might just as easily shoot yourself with that old cannon."

Rolf had his back to me but I could sense his perverse pleasure, "No, I shot 'Expert' with the .45. I hit what I aim at, and if you don't drop that gun belt I might shoot it off."

I was still befuddled and terrified that Rolf was in a vengeful mood and had lost his marbles. *Is this another dream sequence? Is Sister Claudine going to step out of the garage and condemn us all to hell?* Finally I managed to stammer, "What's going on, Rolf?"

"This Sombitch is part of it. We told him about these guys a long time ago and he did nothing. He was almost the first one at Hansen's, and now he shows up here in the middle of the night. Somehow he's connected with these scumbags and that makes him part of Ida's death."

With stunning clarity Rolf had linked the diverse elements of something that had been lost on me.

Then Billy Generaux, let out a loud moan and cried, "I'm hurt, Ed. Help me!"

"Shut up!" Ed yelled. And the full reality of the situation washed over me like a cold shower.

"The gun belt," Rolf repeated, his .45 leveled at Ed Lundquist's body mass

Even from a distance and in the dim light of the early morning, I could see that Ed was sweating, and heavy breathing made his belly heave. He was fairly frothing at the mouth and again his hand started to move toward his holstered pistol but without much conviction. "I'm telling you for the last time. You're interfering with a lawman!"

"No, your just a common criminal," Rolf snarled as he advanced, "and I might shoot you just to shut your yap."

Deputy Lundquist was turning red and hyperventilating as Rolf pushed the .45 into his gut with one hand and unsnapped the pistol belt with the other. "Get down. You know the drill. As Mrs. Odell was fond of saying, 'No rest for the wicked.'" Ed fell to his knees, a loud sob percolated up from his depths, and a growing stain appeared on his trousers as he came to the realization that his criminal enterprise had unraveled.

Night was just beginning to relinquish its hold on the eastern sky when distant sirens and flashing police lights appeared in the east on Highway 37, turning onto Bankers Drive. At that same time there was the *whump-whump-whump* of a helicopter coming across the lake. In less than a minute three squad cars had arrived in the driveway from the east and two black SUVs from the north. County deputies bailed out of the squad cars and four men in black with automatic weapons burst from each SUV. The black Huey, now dominating the scene with its roaring engines, hovered overhead and shone a light not seen since Moses rendezvous on Mount Sinai. The unnatural light with the rapidly deploying police forces produced a surreal spectacle on the quiet lakeside.

We stood spell bound at the unfolding pageant, fearful that a false move could trigger a disaster. Both of us made a show of laying down our weapons. Sheriff Jim Erlansen separated himself from the posse and personally handcuffed Deputy Lundquist, now lying on the ground like a sack of dirty laundry. Then he looked at us, "Stand easy, boys. Sorry we arrived so late, but we couldn't follow Ed too closely without blowing the job. And we didn't know that his two buddies would be here ahead of him, or we would have warned you."

It took ambulance attendants plus several lawmen to get the wailing Billy and the groaning Kenny on gurneys and into the emergency vans. They would live, but Kenny, the executioner, would never be the same again. Neither would Ed Lundquist for that matter. He was better off than the beefy brothers but had lost all his swagger as he was shoved in the back of a police cruiser.

The chopper (FBI as we later learned) doused its light and headed off as daylight began to illuminate the scene. While Rolf mopped up Kenny's blood from the kitchen floor, I cleaned up the broken panel of glass from the back door, then let a frenzied Tina join in the circus. She stopped her scolding bark and got busy greeting the sheriff's men and the Federal Alcohol Tobacco and Firearms and FBI agents, her tail going like an airplane propeller. It was the most fun she'd had since the Fourth.

Rolf, a picture of self-assured contentment, resembled a male Mona Lisa (okay, a really old and far from pretty Mona Liza), but I was still somewhat bewildered by the whirlwind turn of events. I needed a drink, oxygen, a snort of laughing gas. While I had dithered in my reactions and been slow of comprehension, Rolf had risen to the occasion and connected the dots with laser-like instincts. I was Poncho to his Cisco Kid.

Sheriff Erlansen stepped into the cabin with a medic to assess my modest injuries, check on Rolf and help to clear my cobwebs: "Mike, I'll have to pinch you, unless you can stir up a pot of coffee."

I jumped to the task, and while his team finished their investigation, he sat down with us in the kitchen to explain the sequence of events that had culminated here.

It seems that Ed Lundquist and the Generaux boys had been in league for some time. Ed was the brains and the two brothers were the "break and enter" team, no rocket scientists but cunning criminals. Ed would scout likely locations, often with the help of his wife who had access through her real estate activities. After a heist, Ed would provide cover for the burglaries, while the Generauxes would stash the stolen goods, mostly weapons, at various remote locations. One such place was the almost inaccessible island on South Ten Mile Lake where they had paid rent for access. Every few months they would take the stolen guns on the road in the big cargo trailer and fence them to gun shows and dealers far from Minnesota, as distant as Texas. Federal, state, and county law enforcement had suspected Ed Lundquist for some time, but had been reluctant to tip their hand until they could prove their case and bag the whole gang with some strong evidence. Ed was too smart to store stolen goods on his farm but was kept under distant surveillance. When he departed his home in his police cruiser at the unusual hour of 4:00 a.m. the joint strike force went into motion. The law enforcement people had not known the whereabouts of the Generauxes, who lived just across the Red River, and could only hope that Lundquist would lead them to his accomplices. Since Rolf and I were the only people who could identify the brothers, we posed a threat to the gang.

After the throngs had left and things got quiet we treated ourselves to morning beers and sat reflecting on the rapid train of events.

"You were so perceptive and geared for rapid response, and I was so muddled. And again you've saved my tired old ass."

Rolf, as usual a man of few words, "Now it's over. No more lights on the island. Justice for Ida."

"Did you hear the glass in the door when it broke? What got you alerted?"

He pondered for a bit, "I heard something, not sure what. Then I heard Tina growl and heard you tell her to stay. When I saw you take a tumble I grabbed my Colt."

At the sound of her name, Tina perked up and wagged her tail. "Good dog, Tina." Rolf scratched her ears, and Tina got a happy, sloppy look on her face. *He likes me after all.* "She's a loyal one, warning us."

THREE DAYS LATER SHERIFF ERLANSEN called to say that the investigation was wrapped up. The county attorney and a federal prosecutor were preparing indictments. Billy Generaux, who, according to Jim Erlansen, was criminally incompetent, with "less brains than God gave a yellow-rumped warbler," had implicated everyone, even telling police where the stolen merchandise was stashed. "We acted impressed, and Billy took a certain amount of pride in spilling the details of their complex enterprise." Paul Hansen's guns were found with Generaux fingerprints, and their tire impression and shoe prints matched those at Hansens. Ida's blood matched some blood specks found inside the knife scabbard on Kenny's belt.

He added that Kenny was in serious condition but would recover to be tried for murder, along with lesser crimes. Ed Lundquist wanted to plea bargain, but the sheriff and county attorney were not about to give a bad cop any leeway. Both he and his wife would be charged as accessories to murder, attempted murder, and with several counts of grand theft. The feds were drawing up their own list of charges.

TWENTY-NINE

FOR THE NEXT COUPLE OF DAYS we were Zombie-like, still trying to sort out the dramatic events that had overtaken us. It was a giant, continuing story on local TV news, featured in local newspapers and even, we were told, in the Twin Cities papers although we had declined to be interviewed. The latter reports prompted Carol Fellows to call, inquiring if we were all right and to congratulate us on helping to crack the case.

"Let's go over to the resort for dinner," I suggested, "I feel the need of a large piece of cooked meat." Rolf was somewhat reticent but agreed.

I should have known better. All the locals in attendance wanted to chat with us, and we considered a fast exit but soon had free beers in our hands and it would have been impolite to duck out holding one. We got a corner table for two but it didn't help much. I did most the talking as Rolf retreated into his silent refuge and refused eye contact.

When things had finally settled a bit I noted that we were perhaps too famous to go out in public. "Maybe it's time for Meals on Wheels."

"Well at least we don't have to put up with meeting Ed Lundquist here anymore," Rolf pointed out.

That evening as darkness settled over the lake, we were in our customary spot on the deck with Tina, silently contemplating. A pontoon boat of six or eight young folks, strapping boys and leggy girls, eased past our shoreline. We could hear them laughing and caught an occasional word or two. One was pointing toward the cabin and then another raised his voice: "There they are."

Tina lifted her head and cocked her ears towards the intruders, and Rolf emitted an, "Ahc."

One of the young bucks yelled, "Hey, old dudes!" And a young lady called, "Hi, you old dears!" as the entire crew waved.

I had to laugh out loud and waved back. Rolf, despite himself, got a look of wry amusement on his grim face and said, "Never been called an old dude."

"And decidedly not an old dear," I added. "Maybe we should put up Tiki torches to aid the natives in locating us, and sell tickets down on the dock."

"And put a couple of Hula girls on the dock," Rolf added, 'cause we won't be attractions for long." The Andy Warhol syndrome—the clock was ticking on our fifteen minutes of fame.

Despite the good intentions of our friends and neighbors, we failed to find any lasting gratification. We were pleased to see the Lundquist-Generaux mob get its comeuppance, but that didn't balance out Ida's death. The thought of her senseless murder continued to haunt us. Our ruminations on life, death, justice, and mercy got us into some philosophical discussions that we had never entertained in all our hours of wistful thought.

"Do you believe in God, Rolf? Heaven? Hell?"

He sat silently, puffing on his cigar for so long that I thought he might not have heard. Finally he said, "I've had a few glimpses of hell. Guess you have too. Never seen heaven, so I don't know about it. God I'm confused about. If he is everywhere and all merciful, as the preachers say, how could he let Ida down like that? Not to speak of several million Jews in the holocaust? If God is here, I'd sure give a lot for a heart to heart talk with the old boy."

"Well said."

For some years, I had been wrestling with the religious dictums of my youth and the reality of the world. Like Rolf, I had experienced priceless moments of exquisite love and charity, and other times the pervasive cruelty between humans.

It was a brilliantly clear night, now near the end of July, more like the crystal clarity we would get in January. Looking up at the billion-star Milky Way, or what I could see of it through the narrow tunnel of my vision, I marveled at the grandeur of the display. "You know, I'm told that with the naked eye we can only see a fraction of the stars, and even with high-powered telescopes astronomers can't get to the edge of the universe. The enormity of this is all so great that it can't be measured. There are scientists who believe that it could only have been born through some design. I've read about the Big Bang theory, but where did it occur? Even a void has to occupy space and how did that first space come to be? And what keeps all of these planets and galaxies whirling about in some sort of gravitational order? There just must be some higher intelligence."

I glanced at Rolf, and he was looking up with me, his cigar a dull glow in his hand. "That's very profound, Mike. But how can the same God who created this magnificent universe put scumbags like the Generauxes and Ed Lundquist on earth?"

"I'm only guessing. God gave us a free will. At a given crossroads we can do smart things or stupid things. Some of the latter are patently evil. I believe that Jesus walked on the earth. There is so much historic evidence to confirm that. And he preached love and compassion. Though he himself didn't get any. So I guess the almighty can infuse us with right and wrong and put us in play here, but he can't direct our every move or rush to each person's defense when they are about to be victimized. He can preach mercy but he can't dispense it everywhere."

As we pondered that, I recalled another stanza in the Rubaiyat of Omar Khayyam.

The ball no question makes of ayes and noes,
But right or left as strikes the player goes;
And He that toss'd thee down into the field,
He knows about it all—He knows—He knows.

"God must have invented tough love," was Rolf's succinct version of my windy theme. "But if you don't believe God can intercede in events, why do you still go to church?"

"You ask hard questions. Partly I go to pray to my kinsmen. I find comfort in that. And I harbor some uncertainty about my high-blown philosophy. I guess I'm just hedging my bet."

After a lot of additional stargazing, sipping and cigar puffing, Rolf said, "I hope there is a hereafter. I'd like to see my kin again. You know my dad died before I got back from the war. And my mother suffered a great deal. And there's Arnie. Maybe I'll meet them there and tell him how sorry I am for not being there when they needed me."

This was the wrenching undercurrent in his life, the well of guilt and regret. "God, Rolf, don't punish yourself so. You did your damndest. You didn't abandon them. My mother said that everything had to have an explanation. Or does it? It seems that so much of life is random events."

"Still." He stared into the night for a long time, indulging in what I considered his unrealistic expectations.

WE HAD STAYED UP TOO LATE. I had been obliged to wake Tina to get her inside. And it seemed that I had only been asleep for a short time when I was awakened by the touch of her cold wet nose on my arm. When I opened my eyes, looking into hers, I could see she was cocked and primed, communicating to me in silent dog language that she had to go. It was lighter out than usual, and a glance at the alarm clock showed me it was about 7:30 a.m., well past our normal reville. I quickly pulled on slacks and moccasins and got her to the kitchen door and down the steps.

We walked down Bankers Drive while she relieved herself then set about sniffing at all the nocturnal animal traffic. Watching her peeing gave me the urge, but I just had to suck it up because the next part of our morning routine was a retrieving session. Tina pointed at the plastic dummy hanging in the garage and took it on a run down to the lake. When I arrived she relinquished it and stood like a coiled spring on the shoreline awaiting my throw. With a bound that was beyond enthusiastic she propelled herself into the lake and swam to the dummy that I had tossed. Grabbing it like it was alive, she wheeled, using her tail as a sort of rudder, and dog paddled her way back. Just before presenting the object to me, she did a nose to tail-tip shake that sprayed water over half the yard. Then she was ready to go again. Tina never tired of this routine and would have done it until my arm failed or she dropped. I never allowed her to test our limits—three or four tosses were enough.

Back at the house, I got the coffee going and snapped on the TV for local news and weather. After a half-hour of that, it occurred to me that Rolf should have been up by now. Like

Tina, he was a slave to routine and invariably awake by this time. So I poured myself some orange juice, got out some Danish and sat down to read. Our late night of deep philosophy must have tired him as much as it had me.

It was nearing 9:00 a.m. when I noticed the absence of Tina underfoot. I looked about and saw her down the hall lying at Rolf's open bedroom door. *Strange.* She never went in to awaken him as she did me, and she also never camped in his doorway. But she sensed something that was beyond my intellectual powers. With an ill-defined feeling I walked back and looked in on him. Sure enough, the tough old trooper had gone to seek his kin. I summoned the funeral director then sat down with Tina, hugged her and wept bitterly for the loss of our dear friend.

THIRTY

ACCORDING TO THE AUTOPSY, Rolf had died quickly from a massive coronary. It was the latest in a series of bizarre events and left me grieving but stunned. My God, hadn't we earned some peace? I had had trouble getting my thoughts together and needed guidance from Merle Quanrud, the local undertaker. Now six days later, as we headed down I-94 in a black limousine toward the Twin Cities following the hearse, a plan of sorts was unfolding.

There would be no funeral service in the Otter Tail County area. Despite our recent notoriety, people there only knew Rolf as Mike Odell's friend. Rolf had no ties to the community. Merle had suggested a burial at the National Cemetery near the Minneapolis-St. Paul International Airport. It was Rolf's due. And they had placed death notices in both local and Twin Cities' newspapers. My sole task had been to provide evidence that my longtime buddy was in fact a veteran.

I had been obliged to sift through the papers in Rolf's box of private records. There I found a manila jacket containing service records and discharge papers. Among the brittle, crumbling sheets were several citations that Rolf had never alluded to. As I read them the words overwhelmed me: "For conspicuous gallantry in action . . . near Bois de la Haye, France . . . above and beyond the call of duty . . . near Wiltz, Luxembourg . . . with disregard for his personal safety near . . . Colmar, Germany." In the same carton were flat blue boxes that contained several medals:

The Distinguished Service Cross (the nation's second highest award for valor in the face of the enemy), the Silver Star, the Bronze Star, two Purple Hearts for wounds received in action, a Combat Infantry Badge (signifying maximum proficiency as an infantryman) and campaign ribbons. I had listened to the raw details of two of Rolf's combat experiences, but the stories were not self-aggrandizing, as he had related them. I had harbored the suspicion that my old chum was a genuine war hero, but here was the formal documentation, recognition from the U.S. Army.

As I thought about it, the military awards didn't surprise me. Having known Rolf for over fifty years I knew that his personal code would oblige him to do what honor and duty dictated. Rolf had always been embarrassed at expressing his true feelings, was unencumbered by awkward affection, tendencies that had given him an aura of aloofness. But that crusty exterior and his inability to communicate disguised what I knew to be an unfailingly decent man, endowed with nobility.

Tina sat regally beside me in the limo's back seat, off on yet another excellent adventure. The funeral directors had been uncertain about bringing her along, concerned that she would not be allowed into the National Cemetery. But here she was, at my insistence, because she couldn't stay alone at the cabin for seven hours, and because I said *we* were Rolf's next closest living friends. I could imagine Rolf going "Ahc" at such a thought, but in truth, the hardnosed Norwegian had come to love the dog. I had frequently caught him sneaking table snacks to Tina, something the Hansens and I had never condoned. So I reached over and gave her a pet now and then. She was comforting to me, and riding in the back of a black limousine next to her pal, with a stranger at the wheel, she must have been a bit confused, and kept looking down the road, apparently seeking landmarks, trying to ascertain our purpose.

South of Alexandria we passed a billboard for a veterinary supply store that offered the slogan, "Be the man your dog thinks you are."

"Oh, God. How can I explain this to her? I don't understand it myself." She absorbed so much: words, moods, but there was a communication void between man and dog that could not be bridged. You speak and they listen. And the attention they give—as though you were Buddha—and the enthusiastic tail wagging seem to attest to your brilliance. Still, dogs lived for the present. Past events could not be explained to them by human intelligence. She had looked about the cabin for Rolf for the past several days. Would she ever fathom why these people like Paul, Ida, and Rolf had simply dropped from her life? She had me though, and the closer we came to the Cities the closer we clung. We needed each other.

The two-car funeral procession pulled over briefly at a rest stop on the outskirts of Minneapolis while men and dog relieved themselves. Then it was on to the National Cemetery near the airport and old Fort Snelling overlooking the beautiful confluence of the Minnesota and Mississippi rivers.

The gate guard at the cemetery gave me a severe look. "He can't come in, no dogs allowed."

"Well I can't leave *her* outside, and we do have a burial to attend. The two of us are his only family. I'll keep her on a leash and vouch for her good conduct. Otherwise I need to talk to the man in charge." I got a pained look in response, and the guard glanced over his shoulder, and then waved us in.

As we approached the only canopy I could see, there was a cluster of people. *Who could they be?* Several were in identical blue uniforms, an American Legion honor guard that, it turned out, provided a rifle squad for every veteran's burial. There was also a tall, dignified-looking officer in Army dress blues who was a chaplain. Then four old guys in legion caps approached the hearse. I found that they had been acquaintances of Rolf's from his Legion Club on Payne Avenue. They would act as pall-bearers along with the two funeral directors. And then I spotted two beautiful young ladies: the Hansen daughters, Carol and Bonnie. The obituary notice in the *St. Paul Pioneer Press* had caught their eye. Seeing them brought my first flood of tears.

The girls hugged me and each took me by an arm as we followed the flag-draped casket to its resting site. Tina, on her leash next to my leg, was a perfect lady, seeming to under-stand the gravity of the strange doings. With Carol and Bonnie lending their considerable support, we listened as the chap-lain intoned the familiar 23rd Psalm and then the words of John's gospel: "I am the resurrection and the life . . ."

I couldn't help that my mind wandered as I remembered Rolf's joy at my inane plans for an Irish wake and a Viking bur-ial on the lake. And as the chaplain finished, and the amens were said, I muttered, "And may you be in heaven at least a half hour before the devil knows you're gone." It was an Odell family tradition, sacrilegious but both the girls smiled.

At a signal from the chaplain the rifle squad snapped to attention, shouldered rifles, sent off three volleys, then came to present arms. Tina stood, prepared to retrieve any shot ducks, but stayed dutifully at my side, as across the cemetery we heard the mournful strains of Taps:

> Day is done, gone the sun,
> From the hills, from the fields,
> All is well.
> Safely rest, God is nigh.
> All is well.

Rolf would have loved it. Honors rendered, the unchanging traditions. We may not always respect our veterans in life, but we know how to honor them in death.

I wasn't sure if I could bear any more, but we stood like soldiers as the chaplain and the legionnaires slowly and deliberately folded the flag that graced the coffin. Then the officer walked toward us with the triangle of the Stars and Stripes. "Are you his daughters?" the chaplain asked. Both shook their heads and indicated by a nod toward me that I should be the recipient. The tall major looked slightly confused as he refocused.

"I'm his friend, close as he has to family," I managed to say, reluctant to say *we lived together,* not wanting to sully the moment with the weird connotation that phrase had come to have.

Sensing my uneasy fumbling, Bonnie said, "They were like brothers."

The chaplain turned to me, "Then, please accept this flag on behalf of a grateful nation." Rolf had received his final honor. Despite my grief, I knew he must be proud.

I conducted myself well enough to shake hands with the chaplain, the honor guard and the boys from his American Legion post, and accepted their modest words of sympathy, although none of them had known him well. Then there were more hugs from Carol and Bonnie. They said that they would be up to the lake soon and would drop by. "I don't know if I could have managed without one of you on each arm, holding me up. God bless you both."

That grim task behind me, Tina and I, an incongruous pair, got back in our limo for the long, sad trip home.

THIRTY-ONE

THAT EVENING IT CLOUDED over and rain followed some thunder and lightning. It figured. Fit my mood exactly. I was so down. Everything in the cabin reminded me of some shared experience with my old friend. And I couldn't bear to go near Rolf's room. I tried playing some Ella music but her selections all tended toward the blues and did nothing to elevate my melancholy spirits.

I began to realize that the past year, despite some extraordinary events, had been one of the happiest times of my life. Not that Rolf was any barrel of laughs. But he had needed me. He was my set of worry beads. Now he was gone, and my cause, my reason for being had diminished to my own and Tina's humble requirements. Perhaps it was natural that an old guy like me should be so full of self-pity. Each of us, in the time granted tends to think, despite logic, that the world revolves around our petty lives. Yet, if I had a heart attack tomorrow, no one would mourn. Only Tina would be at risk.

I thought of myself in a situation similar to the last of the Knights of the Round Table in Tennyson's, "Morte D'Arthur"

> Then loudly cried the bold Sir Bedivere,
> "Ah! My Lord Arthur, whither shall I go?
> For now I see the true old times are dead . . .
> And I, the last, go forth companionless,
> And the days darken round me . . ."

We only get a few chances to measure up, and mostly we fail. It seemed to me that my life had been largely squandered in limited expectations. I had been involved in no pivotal events. But Rolf was different. He had been a giant among men when it counted, although largely unheralded. He was the soul of modesty, reserved by nature and upbringing, which his years of loneliness had only deepened. Despite his early heroics, I know that he considered himself a failure. Yet success is measured in many ways, and he had doggedly played the cards that fate had dealt.

How was I to get on without him, my buddy, my brother? That night I had more than a few snorts of scotch whiskey and woke late the next morning with a terrible headache. In fact, Tina had been obliged to wake me, and while she conducted her outside business I labored to make a pot of coffee without wrecking the kitchen.

The rain was gone and a rich blue August sky formed a vault over the lake, although I couldn't bear to face the eastern sun for a time. *God, I must have been taking Oban with a syringe, in the ear.*

Tina barked to come in and fussed at me to get going, but I sat for a some time looking over the lake watching the mist dissipate. She gave me a gentle head butt on the leg and I looked down into those brown eyes that reached back into my soul. Then she did a pirouette toward the door, looking back at me and wagging hard, "Come on. Let's get on with it." I knew she was right, my four-legged therapist. I had to climb out of this well of remorse and self-pity. Either it or the scotch would put me in the loony bin.

So, following some retrieving exercises at the lake, after which Tina shook water all over me, and after pumping last night's rain from the boat, I planned my endless yard mowing duties. Coffee and fresh air had begun to clear my head. With a riding mower you need to focus on what you're doing or risk an accident, so as best I could, I banished Rolf from my mind and paid attention to grass cutting. Tina followed at a respectful distance, periodically lying down in the new mown grass and rolling on her back.

I was just finishing Hansen's yard when a strange sedan appeared in my driveway. Tina was loping toward the car as a strapping young man stepped out. He put his hand out cautiously and allowed Tina a sniff, and then she began wagging her tail. She had welcomed him but damned if I could figure out who it was. He had a rugged build, a man who could take care of himself.

I pulled the John Deere mower into the yard, stopped it near the garage and stepped off. I was a bit wary. Too many unpleasant surprises had me spooked. And yet there was a deja vue sensation, something vaguely familiar about him. I guessed he was in his late forties, and my first thought was that he might be a police officer still investigating the Lundquist gang caper, but the car was unmarked and unremarkable. He was about six-foot-three with a superbly muscular build, close-cropped blonde hair and penetrating blue eyes and looked like he could be dangerous, although exhibiting no hostile intent, and was busy scratching Tina's ears. Her instinct was one of total acceptance. He wore khaki slacks and then I noted his T-shirt that said "Army."

As I walked toward him, he stretched out a hand, no doubt noting my concern. "Sir, would you be Mr. Odell?" My hand was engulfed in a firm but friendly grip. He smiled slightly and once again I had a flicker of recognition.

"Yes, I'm Mike Odell."

"A real estate agency in St. Paul gave me your address. I tried to call yesterday and this morning but got no answer. I was told I might find Rolf Holt here." I didn't answer right away, displaying my customary befuddlement. So he forged ahead. "I'm Arnie Bell. I believe I might be Rolf Holt's son."

My confusion popped like a soap bubble. "Of course you are." You could have knocked me over with a wet noodle. Before me stood Rolf Holt, the new and improved version.

My heart was trying to pound its way out of my chest, and that old sphincter or whatever it was in my throat that tightened and rendered me unaccountably dumb when overcome with emotion, began gagging me. I just managed to say, "Come in," as I struggled to get myself under control.

I invited him to sit down and asked if he would like a cold drink. "Whatever you have," he said politely.

"How about a cold beer?" I was sweating from being in the sun and from the anxiety of the dreamlike meeting.

"That would be fine," he said, glancing about for anyone else.

I was struggling with how to tell him about Rolf's passing, when he thrust a paper at me. "You probably have questions about me. Here is something that may explain my quest and satisfy you that it's legitimate."

His striking resemblance to Rolf had been sufficient, but I took the proffered document, while my brain got into gear. It was a worn birth certificate, covered with laminate, from the City of St. Paul, dated October 28, 1946. It was for Arnold Holt, and the parents were listed as Rolf and Ella Holt, at the address on the east side that I knew so well.

As I was studying this ancient piece of history, long forgotten images of fifty years ago flashed in my memory. He broke my reverie by saying; "My foster parents got hold of this somehow and saved it until I was old enough to understand."

I nodded, although still awash in confusion. He went on: "As nearly as I know, I was adopted by a childless couple, James and Anna Bell when I was about two. I don't know what happened to my real mother, and of course have no recollection of her. But the Bells raised me as their own, and had always intended to tell me about the adoption, but it sort of slipped until a few of years ago when my mom died. My father, a minister in the Carolinas, had passed away two years before. My mother remembered this birth certificate and gave it to me before she died of cancer. It made no difference to me, since they were the only parents I had ever known and had raised me in a house of love and understanding, along with two other adopted children, that I came to believe were my blood sisters. But recently I started to become curious about my background and found some time to investigate the details on that birth certificate. I never had any real hope of finding anything, rather assumed that my real parents were both dead by now, and the address on the birth certificate had to be a long shot."

I took a deep breath before I attempted to answer his forthright story. "Well, you're one hell of a detective. Your dad was rooted to that very house until a year ago. He had some notion that you and your mother might return there some day. Seemed crazy to me. But damned if he wasn't right. I don't know about your mother. Your father lost track of her after she returned south to visit her people with you in 1947. He stayed in St. Paul at the Holt home hoping the two of you would return. His father was dead, his mother ill, and he felt he had obligations here. Ella never returned, and he lost track of her. Phone calls and letters went unanswered. He never knew what had happened to the two of you. But I can attest that he carried a ton of guilt for his lifetime that he had lost track of you."

I took a swig of cold beer and plodded on. "Rolf and I were friends since high school, and he came to live with me about a year ago. It was a happy time for him, and for me, but just a week ago he died here of a massive heart attack." Now that I had gotten to the punch line I could not hold back a few tears and a sob or two.

Arnie put a hand on my shoulder, and said softly, "I'm sorry, I've lost good close friends and loved ones too. And I know about obligations, duties that sometimes can dominate our lives. I've just retired after thirty years in the Army." The stalwart young man was dry eyed. It took me a moment to understand that he could hardly weep for a man he never knew. But I determined to rectify that.

From Rolf's room I brought out his pitiful few mementoes: family photos and his service records. Arnie studied the faded black-and-white pictures of people who had given him life but were a total mystery to him. He grinned as he tapped at Rolf's image of fifty years ago. "It's like looking in a mirror."

I nodded and went on, "I had to find his military service records to qualify him for the national cemetery near the Twin Cities Airport. Look at them."

As he perused the citations I laid out the blue boxes containing the medals.

"My God!" Arnie said. "He was a bona fide hero: DSC, Silver Star, Bronze Star, and two purple Hearts. What a guy."

"And that's just one chapter in his life. Let me tell you what he's done lately." I recounted the rescue of the kid in the ice last winter, and then the saga of the bad guys that had invaded the neighborhood and Rolf's determined efforts to bag the lot. Arnie listened in wonder at the lengthy tale and the final scene.

It seemed that we had only talked for a short time but suddenly it was 6:00 p.m. All I had offered Arnie was a couple of cold beers in that time. "Well, I guess I should be going.

You've been very nice, Mister Odell, and I don't want to wear out my welcome."

"For God sake, how could you do that? It's been fifty years between visits. Do you have to catch a plane?"

"No, not until tomorrow afternoon. But I don't want to be a burden."

I rolled my head back and let out a laugh. "That's exactly what your dad said when he left St. Paul to live here. "I've got so much more to tell you. Stay the night at least."

"Well, thanks. I can't tell you how much this has meant to me."

"Son, for me your appearance is like winning the lottery. And quit calling me Mr. Odell. I was your godfather. I'm just Mike to you. Have you ever had walleyed pike?"

"No, but I hear it's the filet mignon of fish.'

"Then I'll cook some that your dad caught. Have a before-dinner beer."

After a classic Ten Mile Lake supper, we strolled down to the lake and gave Tina some retrieving exercise. Arnie delighted in seeing her catapult off the shore into the lake for the dummy. I told him how his dad had slowly warmed to Tina and grown to love her. As I spoke of her, Tina nuzzled me and said, "Uh, uh, uh."

"She's a real buddy, isn't she," Arnie observed.

"Yes, a loyal friend. And your dad placed great stock in loyalty."

We had a boat ride, and for the first time Arnie really got a chance to see the lake and marveled at its beauty and diversity. Returning to the dock, I showed him Rolf's tackle box with all his lures, including the giant plug with the spectacles.

Before we settled down I showed Arnie the potato cannon that Rolf had labored over. The professional soldier grinned in a way that crinkled the crow's feet around his eyes and warmed my heart with images of another.

We sat on the deck that warm August evening, as I had done so often with Rolf, and I introduced Arnie to Oban scotch. "Tell me about yourself. Retired from the Army you said."

He had enlisted after high school graduation to earn some money for college, had fought in Vietnam then returned to the States and been sent to Officer Candidate School. After earning his commission, he saw additional combat in Panama, Bosnia, and the Gulf War. The Army had seen to it that he got his college degree in computer science along the way. After thirty years of active service he had recently retired with the rank of colonel, and was now scouting for a job that utilized his high tech background. He had interviewed with two firms in the Twin Cities area just before setting off on his quest.

"Oh, but your dad would be proud of how much you have accomplished. Tell me about your family."

"I married Tricia, an Army brat, in 1970." As he spoke he broke out a family photo from his wallet that showed a lovely wife and two fine looking kids. "We have a son and a daughter. Ben is twenty-three and serving in the Army, and Janie is eighteen and about to enter college, and, boy, is it expensive. Uncle Sam is taking care of Ben's education."

"Well now. That puts me in mind of something else we haven't gotten around to talking about. Rolf has planned for his granddaughter's college expenses." Arnie blinked, a quizzical look on his face. I was having a great time. "He has near $50,000 in savings here, and as executor of his estate I hereby declare it to be used for Janie's education and for whatever else you deem appropriate."

Arnie swallowed a snort of Oban. "My God! I can't believe it. But didn't he intend that money for you, Mike?"

"Of course he did, and if I went first he would get my worldly possessions. But what am I going to use it for? This place is my Shangri-la. And my retirement pay is sufficient for my needs. I can't think of anything that I could buy that would give me as much pleasure as helping your family. But, there's one condition. You've got to come back and see me and bring the family."

"That's an easy requirement. I love this North Country and am going to do everything I can to locate here. But I promise I'll be back to visit no matter what."

He called home that evening and told his wife of his success. Then, I talked to Tricia briefly. She sounded as sweet as she looked from the snapshot.

As Arnie left the next day, I felt like I had known him for years. He reached out a strong hand to shake goodbye, and I gave in to my long-standing urge to hug a Holt. "Your dad did not approve of such emotional outbursts." Then I teared up as he climbed into his car.

Arnie got a concerned look, "Are you okay, Mike?"

"Yes, I'm fine. As you get older you'll find that most organs seem to fail or sag, your tear ducts are at full throttle. I can cry when I flip an over-easy egg without breaking it."

He gave me an understanding smile, a smart salute, and headed for I-94.

Just yesterday, I had wondered how I could carry on. My main reason for being seemed to have vanished. Tina was my only anchor to windward.

Then Arnie had appeared and he and his family were my manifest destiny, my unfinished business. I began to fantasize their visits, wonder if the cabin needed improvements to accommodate them. I could almost hear Rolf saying, "Ahc," at such wishful thinking, for I had always been the dreamer while he was firmly grounded in the reality of the moment. Still my formerly dismal life now had a chapter yet to unfold. And I could only look forward with undisguised joy.

That evening, as the sun set on South Ten Mile Lake, I sat with Tina at my side to revel in the appearance of Arnie and all it might mean. And as old guys do, I ruminated on whether Rolf was looking down and felt compelled to raise my glass to him in the heavens. "Here's to you in your Valhalla. God love you, Rolf, for being my friend."

Tina raised her head to see what I might be marking and added, "Uh, uh, uh."